THE
EYE
OF THE
HUNTER

AN EVANS NOVEL OF THE WEST

THE
EYE
OF THE
HUNTER

FRANK BONHAM

Thorndike Press • Thorndike, Maine

Library of Congress Cataloging in Publication Data:

Bonham, Frank.
  The eye of the hunter / Frank Bonham.
  p. cm.
  ISBN 0-89621-891-0 (alk. paper : lg. print)
  I. Title.
[PS3503.O4315E94   1989b]   89-27490
813'.54--dc20   CIP

Thorndike Press Large Print edition published in 1989 by arrangement with M. Evans & Company, Inc.

Cover design by James B. Murray.

This book is printed on acid-free, high opacity paper. ∞

PART ONE

THE GUNSMITH

Chapter One

Nogales, Arizona Territory: May 1900

In three punishing days of train travel, Henry Logan had had plenty of time to think about Richard Parrish and his pretty wife. He thought the man must be dead, although the Richard I. Parrish trust checks were faithfully cashed each month — by someone whose handwriting looked to him more like a woman's than a man's. But Rip Parrish, an inveterate gambler and letter writer, had not answered a letter in nearly a year.

An attorney named John Manion, in Kansas City, wanted Logan find out why, although he was neither a Pinkerton man nor a lawyer. He was a gunsmith, and he served Manion's collection of firearms. He was also a Spanish-American War vet, still under the weather from the malaria he had brought home from Cuba, and Manion thought the trip to Arizona might be good for his health. The trust would pay all Logan's expenses, and he would certainly cost less than a Pinkerton man. All the detective work he would need to do if Parrish wasn't around, the lawyer said, was to check the cemeteries and Hall of Records for traces of the man.

And of course find and interview his pretty wife.

Nothing was ever as easy as it was made out to be, Logan knew, but the job sounded interesting. In a way it would be like going home. He had lived for two years with his parents at Fort Bowie, in southeastern Arizona, before his father's death. But that was nine years ago. His recollections of the country were vague, and he had never been in Nogales.

What finally persuaded him to take the job, he realized, was that Parrish's young wife, Frances, was apparently a real beauty. He had made himself an authority on Frances by studying the wedding picture the man had sent a couple of years ago. It made a lot of sense, of course, for him to be traveling halfway across the country mainly to find out whether she was as beautiful as she appeared in the picture. But he had come back from the war with some firm convictions, one of which was that if you really felt like doing something, you'd better do it now, before destiny intervened. Maybe, if Parrish was dead, she was as lonesome as he was. Maybe she liked gunsmiths.

So here he was this morning, dazed with fatigue, gaunt and unshaven in a wrinkled black suit he had not worn since before the war, gazing through a dusty window as the train clattered alongside an almost dry wash striped with rivulets and sandbars and called the Santa Cruz River. The conductor had advised the half dozen passengers of the mixed train to collect their belongings, and they were staggering around closing valises and hampers and putting on hats.

Henry remained seated. He was traveling light, with only a barracks bag and a case of gunsmith's tools. It had been years since he had seen country as dry as this. The mountains in the distance were fantastically shaped, knoblike, jagged, lumpy, and protuberant, while the hills bordering the river valley looked as though they had been pinched up out of wet clay. Here and there yellow cane thickets grew along the streambed, and there were small olive-gray trees as well as a variety of cactus that looked like terrible whips tipped with blood. Yet the earth had a pretty, rosy tinge, and the whole area a bizarre beauty.

The train began a harsh clanking and convulsive shuddering. Coal smoke settled upon the cars and drifted in through the crevices. Henry craned his neck to see what was going on. Directly ahead, the railroad tracks split a shallow bowl in which a town lay protected by two barricades of brown hills piled up like earthworks. Overhead, the sky was a clear cornflower blue. The entire community, except for the business district, was perched on the hillsides — hovels on the east, somewhat larger homes with tin roofs on the west. Absolutely everythng was constructed of the only building material he had noticed in the Territory: dirt. The dirt was formed into adobe bricks and, sometimes, plastered. The plaster did not adhere well: Many of the buildings looked like Missouri hogs with patches of dried mud on their sides.

With a squalling of iron shoes, the train came to a shuddering stop. Henry sat a moment gathering strength. In the sudden quiet, his ears rang. He realized he was overdue for a draft of quinine. Finally he got up and carried his bags forward. The last passenger off the train, he stood leaning against a baggage cart until he caught the eye of a man with a long-spouted oilcan.

"I've got a horse back there," he said. "Big red dun?"

"Right. They'll bring it to the hitch rack, yonder."

"Keep an eye on him, would you? I don't want him going on to Mexico." He gave the man a silver dollar and a wink. Traveling on someone else's money was proving to be a great improvement on paying your own way.

Already, in May, it was pretty warm, but when he entered the waiting room he found it surprisingly cool. Adobe, he knew, had the fine insulating qualities of a cave. He sat on a bench against the wall while the half dozen other passengers lined the counter, asking questions of a man in a green eyeshade. Could he recommend a hotel? Was there a good restaurant? At the near end of the counter, a man with a gray fedora on the side of his head was writing a telegram. Henry was supposed to wire John Manion of his arrival, but it could wait. He felt a little feverish; it was past time for his quinine. He would take the awful stuff as soon as he was installed in a boardinghouse.

The building seemed to lurch. Was it swaying, or was his body still bracing itself against the jouncing of the railroad train? He decided everything was all right, and almost immediately his limbs sank into a blissful torpor. He felt as though he were moored in a little backwater in which he did not have to decide things, worry about the aftereffects of malaria, and wonder about what had happened to Rip Parrish.

Lately he had been worrying too much about too many things. He was twenty-two. He had come to lanky maturity on a farm in Missouri, spent a year and a half in the Army in Cuba, serving first as an armorer, then as a sharpshooter; and although the Spanish troops had failed to hurt him, a mosquito had brought him down with a single shot of its small-bore stinger.

On the walk outside the shop he heard two women talking. In a tree a cicada was creating a hypnotic drone. *Hold on,* he thought, confused. *The shop? Come on, Henry! — your gun shop, in Kansas City, Missouri.*

Kansas City? Wait a minute, boy — where are you?

. . . He was in his gun shop on a side street in Kansas City, Missouri. He must be there — he could smell the good banana-like fragrance of gun oil. He had just handed to a customer, a lawyer named John Manion whose collection of firearms he serviced, a black-powder model Colt he had left for repair. Manion liked to hear him tell about sharpshooting in Cuba, and how, as an armorer, he had personally taken care of Colonel Teddy Roosevelt's famous '95 Winchester.

The lawyer tested the hammer clicks of the

revolver. "That's better. What was the problem, Henry?"

Logan explained that a tang on the hammer mechanism was worn smooth. He said he could have refiled it but thought it was a better idea to replace the whole piece.

"What do I owe you?"

"Dollar'll do it. Could I offer you an Irish blessing, for the road?"

Manion accepted, and from under the counter Henry Logan took a bottle of Irish whiskey and two glasses. While he poured the whiskey, the lawyer opened his briefcase and began sorting and searching until finally he pulled out what looked like a studio photograph in a gray folder. He tossed it on the counter.

"Take a look at this," he said. Was there something sly in his smile? He watched with amusement while Logan opened the folder and gazed blankly at an ordinary wedding photograph. Turning the picture over, Logan read the photographer's stamp on the reverse: Y. GUERRERRO. NOGALES, A.T.

Then he studied the members of the wedding again. "Am I supposed to know these folks, John?"

"No, but the groom's a client of mine. Take another look. Ever see a wedding picture before where the groom was wearing a hat and holding a gun? Damned featherbrain. *Rich* featherbrain," he added.

Intrigued, Henry held the photograph under a goosenecked lamp. The bridegroom was big and handsome in a fringed leather coat. He wore a trimmed jawline beard and mustache and a wide grin. A sombrero was pushed to the back of his head. And Henry chuckled when he realized that the man held at port arms a long-barreled Colt. The pose, and the groom's waggish expression, made him think of an outlaw who had stopped running long enough to get himself married and have his picture taken.

"Isn't that rare?" Manion asked.

"I'm surprised the bride let him get away with it. What's he do?"

"Nothing, as far as I know. Plays at being a rancher. Actually, he's the nephew of a client I had, a gambler named Humboldt Parrish. Hum won a ranch near Nogales in a poker game. When he died, couple of years ago, the nephew inherited it and got married. Richard I. Parrish — known as Rip, and the grin tells you why."

And the bride, Henry supposed, would be a suitable mate for a man who carried a gun and wore a hat at his own wedding. Yet when he looked more closely, he murmured in surprise. For she was truly a beauty, and no saloon

14

beauty, either. The top of her head came to her husband's ear. She stood straight and slender in a puff-sleeved dress that was tight in the waist and full-bosomed, with a high lace collar closed by a cameo — the "something old," maybe. Still, her gown was for street wear, not for a church wedding. Small crosses hung from her earlobes, and a tortoiseshell comb rose from the back of her head like a peacock's tail.

"Got a magnifying glass?" Manion asked. "Take a look at that gun! An 1873 Army Colt, engraved and gold-inlaid and with a genuine ruby in the front sight! We fired a couple of rounds when Rip was in town — just stuck it out the window and let fly at the river!"

Logan found a magnifying glass in a drawer full of tools.

"Squint hard and maybe you can see the ruby," Manion said.

Logan squinted. "I can't, but I can sure see Rip's diamond. She's a thousand-dollar presentation model herself! Does she look a litte foreign, maybe? What's the word? Exotic . . ."

"Maybe. Her father was a doctor in Arizona, but he practiced in Sonora for years. So maybe she picked up the look, somehow. Rip called her Panchita — Spanish for Frankie. Her name's Frances. Kind of taken by her?" asked the lawyer, amused.

"Well, you know . . ." Logan said. "The beautiful face in a crowd thing — ever had that experience? You think, You gorgeous creature, what are you doing on some other man's arm? And look at her expression, John — is that independence, or haughtiness, or . . . what?"

"Disdain," said Manion. "Disdain for her hoorawing husband, clowning for his own wedding picture."

"So why did she marry him?"

"She's probably wondering that herself, by now. Especially," said the lawyer, "since he seems to be missing. Cashes his trust checks but hasn't answered a letter since last summer."

"If he's like me, he probably hates writing letters."

"He didn't used to. And there are always questions about his trust that I've got to have answers to. How does he want his money invested? Does he want to sell that stock? Buy a little farmland? But he doesn't write to say boo anymore."

"Ask his wife."

"She doesn't write, either. But somebody's cashing those checks, Henry. Not Rip, because the handwriting is different. Look at this. . . ."

16

From his coat Manion took an envelope. He drew out a couple of bank drafts and laid them before the gunsmith. "Before and after," he said.

The difference was clear. The earlier check, dated August 1898, was signed with a bold flourish. On the later one, dated two months ago, the name *Richard I. Parrish* was traced in the same calligraphic swirls and brown ink as the names on the back of the photograph.

"As the administrator of the trust, I've got to do something pretty soon. Find out whether R.I.P. stands for his initials, or 'rest in peace.'"

"Send a Pinkerton man," Henry suggested.

"Cost an arm and a leg." Manion sipped his whiskey and regarded Henry with a grin. And suddenly Henry saw where this whole charade was leading. He laid the magnifying glass down and gave a chuckle.

"Okay, John, I get it. You think a change of climate might be good for me."

"I really do. You were off two days last week, and you still look like parchment. A trip might do you a world of good. The trust would pay all your expenses, and a couple of hundred to boot. As a bonus, you'll be interviewing Frances Parrish and finding out what she's really like. Can she bake a cherry pie? Does she like to dance? The detective work should be like shooting fish. If Rip's dead, he'll be enshrined in a Hall of Records somewhere. Not to mention a cemetery."

"Think about, Henry. Do us both a favor. Well, I'm off."

The lawyer had only gotten as far as the door when Henry said, "I've thought about it. When would you like me to leave?"

The lawyer wanted him to leave as soon as possible. A few days later he gave him a folder of correspondence, the wedding picture, and a power of attorney. He provided him with a money belt with a supply of gold pieces, and a railroad ticket. He said, "The picture might help you identify Rip Parrish if you find him in a shallow grave. I don't know whether he wrote a will in Nogales, but he left none here, so if he's dead, the bride is pretty well fixed."

"If you feel so good in Arizona that you decide to stay, I'll have your stuff crated and shipped."

The night before he left, Henry studied the features of Frances Wingard Parrish. The more he looked at her, the more captivated he was. He liked the quirk of her eyebrows, and thought her throat the most graceful line he had ever seen on a woman. But then he thought, wryly, Mrs. Rip, you wouldn't kill your husband for his ranch, would you?

That would be beyond belief. Yet it was also hard to believe that Rip would cash his checks but not answer his mail. Something was going on out there, and one person who was sure to know what it was, was Frances Parrish.

Chapter Two

"Mr. Logan?"

Henry opened his eyes. A man wearing a green eyeshade was peering at him from behind a counter. For a moment he was unable to decide where he was.

"Mr. Henry Logan?" the man said, with a sympathetic smile. He was tall and thin, with a small head decorated with black hair slicked down and parted in the middle.

"Hello," Henry said.

"Your horse is at the rack, now, my friend. Are you . . . everything okay?"

Henry took a lungful of the warm, dusty Arizona air that was supposed to put him back on his feet. The cicada that had put him into a trance was a telegraph key at the end of the counter. "I'm fine," he said. By a considerable effort, he managed to get on his feet and tried to think of what came next. He had saved a question to ask after the other passengers were finished with theirs. They had all departed now, and he heard his horse pawing the ground at the rack outside, relieved to be out of a railroad car after three days on the road.

"I'd like to find a nice, quiet boarding-house," he said. "Not too expensive."

The stationmaster called to another man down the counter, who appeared to be writing a telegram.

"What do you think, Ben? A boarding-house."

Henry turned his head to look at the man, who unhurriedly finished something he was writing, handed it to the telegrapher, and then turned to look coolly at Henry. He held a black cigarillo fore and aft in his teeth, his lips flared back from long, stained yellow teeth. He looked like a small-town dandy, the edges of his long gray coat banded in black, a curl-brimmed gray fedora on the side of his head, the tips of his full gray mustache waxed. Yet his face had an outdoor look, stringy and brown, like beef jerky. He studied Henry for a moment, puffing on the Mexican cigarette.

"What did you have in mind, friend?" he asked. "Semipermanent?"

"Two or three weeks. Maybe more."

The man turned to the telegrapher. "How much do I owe you?" He paid him in big silver coins, adjusted his necktie, and came to pick up one of Henry's army bags. He offered his hand, smiling, cigarette still in his long front teeth.

"Ben T. Ambrose," he said. "I publish the *Globe*, the evening paper."

"Henry Logan."

"Logan!" the man said. He turned back to the telegrapher. "Didn't you have somethng for Mr. Logan, Tom?"

"Sure did." The telegrapher searched through some pigeonholes and found a small brown envelope, which Ambrose took from his hand and handed to Henry with some formality.

Henry was surprised, and felt important. It was from Manion, of course. He tucked the small brown envelope in the inside pocket of his wrinkled black coat. Ambrose was looking at him as though trying to recall his face. Finally he said, "A woman named Alice Gary has a nice place up on the hill. She's an excellent cook, and it's only a few blocks from the center of town. Out of the dust, too."

"That's what I would have said," the stationmaster agreed.

Then why didn't you? Henry wondered. Apparently the editor was someone to be deferred to.

Suddenly Ambrose said: "Logan! If you were older, I'd say you were the brother of

22

Black Jack Logan. The resemblance is fantastic."

Henry smiled. "I'm his son."

"Well, I'll be damned!"

His hand was in the editor's lean claw again, being crushed this time. "Welcome to hell's half acre, Henry! Met your father several times when he was posted to Bowie. Fine man — died a hero. Soldier's Medal, wasn't it?"

"Yes."

"I gave Black Jack a half page in my book. Have you read it? *On the Border with Stockard: Taming the Savage Apache.*"

"Yes, I know it. Funny about medals, though. Do a chapter on them sometimes. Dead officers die heroes and get medals. Dead troopers are dead troopers and get buried."

"Wrong! I could give you a list of enlisted heroes as long as your arm —"

"Not at Murphy's Barn, though. Eight dead troopers, one dead officer. Guess who got the medal?"

"You were twelve years old then, Henry! They may have suppressed some of the facts to spare your mother. He was tortured! They tried to make him tell where he'd hidden the payroll box. He didn't tell, either. He died to save it."

Henry smiled. It was amazing how people would believe what they wanted to. The

Black Jack Logan myth, for instance, was one he himself had believed, until last year when a letter had arrived from Central America. . . .

"How do I find Mrs. Gary's place?" Henry asked.

Ambrose settled his hackles and grumbled. "I'll take you myself. Where are you from, Logan?"

"Kansas City."

"Here on business?"

"Health. I'd appreciate the ride, but what I need first is a beer, a bath, and a barbershop. In that order."

Ambrose looked closely at Henry's yellowish face. "Liver?"

"Malaria. Every now and then I have a little spell. A friend thought I ought to try Arizona."

Ambrose nodded. "A friend indeed! The desert will put you back on your feet. Beer — you can get good steam beer in the hotel across from my office, and there's a barbershop also where you can soak out your miseries. I'll leave you and the horse there and take your gear on up to Allie's."

"Thank you very much."

Outside, Ambrose put the bags in a buggy while Henry tied his horse to the rig. Henry felt guilty about spoiling the editor's Black Jack Logan scene.

"Ben, I'm sorry about the medal business. But in Cuba, death was the real thing. Nobody gave a damn about medals after a day or two under fire. Sherman was right about Cuba, too."

"Of course. War was hell in Arizona, too."

Ambrose shook the reins and they headed up the main street. The editor handled the buggy as ostentatiously as though he were the grand master of a parade, reins held high, his pencillike cigarette pointing the way, and Henry noticed that a number of people waved at him from the walks. He would return the greeting with a salute of a fringed glove.

"What do you do in Kansas City?" he asked.

"I'm a gunsmith."

"Where'd you get the malaria?"

"Cuba. I was an armorer," Henry said.

"Then you missed all the real excitement, eh?"

Henry looked at him. He was grinning ferociously, showing his teeth. "No, sir," he said. "I had it both ways — at a bench and under fire. Colonel Roosevelt watched me zero in his pet rifle one day — a '95 Winchester. I never bench-fired them, I just hauled off and tore out the bull's-eye, offhand. He was so impressed with my marksmanship that he put me in a tree with a rifle and a telescope."

"Indeed! The great Colonel Roosevelt personally made you a sharpshooter?"

"I suppose God made me a sharpshooter. Colonel Roosevelt only made me a sniper."

Ambrose's laugh was like a snarl. "That's good," he said. "You can take the ash off a mosquito's cigarette at a hundred yards, that what you mean?"

"I mean that shooting comes natural to me."

"You're bragging." Ambrose was teasing.

Henry shrugged. "No. I'm not bragging."

As the buggy jounced on its soft town-springs along the street between the flinty little hills, he tried to decide why Nogales was supposed to be so good for the health. Well, the air, he supposed, which though dusty went into the lungs easily, light and warm and dry. Maybe a bit too dry: His skin itched.

Nogales intrigued him. The town had an air of age as well as modernity — the oldest building material in the world meeting cement sidewalks and telephone poles cobwebbed with wires. A few structures were of mellow-looking red bricks, while most of the roofs were tin, or flat and hidden behind parapets.

"What do you think of our town?" asked Ambrose.

"I like it. It looks as foreign as Cuba, though."

"Got a Mexican accent," Ambrose agreed. "Fine little town, though. Gateway to Guaymas, the Sonora seaport. Altitude thirty-six eighty-nine. Population over twenty-five hundred. That's my shop," he said, pointing.

Henry looked left. Directly across from a large hotel was a steep and narrow building with a flagpole protruding from the roof and a golden globe hanging by a chain from the pole. On the globe, in black, were the words:

THE ARIZONA GLOBE
B. AMBROSE, PUB. & ED.

"The gilt on that globe is genuine Arizona gold, mined fifteen miles from here."

"Handsome. Does it ever need polishing?"

"Never. Does your wife's wedding ring?"

"No. It might if I were married."

"Of course you know the name of Miles Stockard," Ambrose said.

"The Indian-fighting general?"

"Right. He lives here in town, too. Matter of fact, he's my partner in a small way. Fine old gentleman, eye like a hawk, made a sharpshooter out of every man in his outfit. It's all in my book."

Henry had despised the author's contemptuous attitude toward Indians, as though they were some sort of game to be tracked and

27

shot. He also knew something about fine old officers with eyes like hawks. In Cuba, one had sent his squad out on a night patrol to bring back a prisoner — for the idiotic reason that it was his wife's birthday. They had brought back no prisoners, but one of the squad was badly wounded.

Ben Ambrose, pub. and ed., reined in his horse before a two- story building with verandas. The sign above the wooden awning read, *FRONTERA HOTEL.* Ambrose offered his gloved hand and another fierce, yellow-fanged grin. "Drop in sometime, Logan. I'll stuff your craw full of local history. Not going to read your telegram?"

"I'm saving it to read with my beer."

"You'll find the bar on your right as you enter. I suggest carrying your beer into the baths — I'd recommend two beers, Logan, judging by your color!" He gave the sharp, snarling laugh again.

Henry tied his big army horse before the hotel as Ambrose drove off with his baggage.

The Frontera Hotel was thronged with ranchers, cowboys, army men in polished boots, and men who might be mining engineers, wearing hard-brimmed army-style hats and clean work clothing. Someone was playing a piano. There were no women. Here and there two or three men seemed to be huddling over business matters. The oiled wooden floor was patterned with vivid Mexican rugs, and the tall narrow windows were hung with net drapes. The room smelled of floor oil and tobacco smoke. Overhead, a ceiling fan turned silently.

Henry passed through a door into the bar, bought two steam beers, and carried them into the barbershop. An old Mexican man with white revolutionary-style mustaches led him into a room in the rear with three big zinc tubs.

While the old man and a boy filled his tub, bucket by steaming bucket, Henry undressed to his underwear and sat on a stool. He started on the first beer. Cold and clear and red, it flowed down his throat like a blessing. He sighed. Then, feeling restored, he dug the telegram out of his coat pocket. It was from John Manion, and had been sent the day after he left Kansas City: "Mrs. Parrish writes husband missing. Circumstances dictate caution. Advise discuss with her only."

Henry thought, Aha! The fact that Parrish had not personally cashed his checks for eight months had to mean that he was unable to — because of illness or absence. Clearly John's last letter, threatening to turn off the money spigot, had accomplished its purpose, jarring the widow or wife off dead center.

He sipped some more beer. So his business was going to be with Frances Parrish. He wished he knew more about her, how to approach her without antagonizing her and putting her on guard. Since the tub was not ready, he opened his leather portfolio and found Parrish's first letter to John, dated nearly three years ago.

> My wife is quite the horsewoman, and a dead shot. She used to go everywhere with her father, who was a country doctor, so the back woods of this ranch don't scare her. The canyons are crawling with mountain lions, smugglers, and thieves, but Panchita, as the maid calls her, goes right out there, alone, to look for lost cows. . . .

Again, Henry scrutinized the wedding picture. Could hints to the woman's nature be found there? The fact that the studio was in Sonora, that her gown was pretty but informal, suggested some rather hasty arrangements, a spur-of-the moment wedding. Shotgun, maybe? No: At least Rip had scarcely hit Nogales when he had married her. He tried to see in her face the brush-popping frontierswoman, but her arrestingly pretty features defeated him. The face was flawless — in his opinion — her hair brushed back and waved in the style of a Greek marble, her eyebrows dark and arched; the pale eyes would have to be gray or blue. They quirked up a little at the corners-charming, he thought! Exotic! Physically, she looked to be a lightweight; but frail little women had been manipulating men since Eve. Though it was almost impossible to believe, she might be a husband killer.

A dead shot, as Rip had said. . . .

The old man called something in Spanish.

Henry slipped into the hot water with a sigh of pleasure. Soaping, he tried to recall in Rip's last letter a forecast of trouble breeding like a germ. Some trivia — a slight fever, harbinger of a lethal disease; an angry encounter with someone. But he remembered nothing of that sort.

Rip was missing, and Mrs. Rip was willing to talk about it. But only to him, evidently. And he would bet his money belt that she had a story to tell, too. . . .

Chapter Three

Nogales, A.T.: August 1899

Frances Parrish was saddling her little buckskin mare in the yard of the ranch house fifteen miles up the Santa Cruz River. She wore a divided leather skirt for the long ride ahead, a frilled white shirt of her father's, and blued Chihuahua spurs on her boots. Her dark hair was pinned up because of the heat, with a straw boater atop it.

Her old Mexican maid, Josefina, held the bridle of her horse as she tied a blanket roll behind the cantle. She had known Josefina since she was a child in Hermosillo. The women chattered breathlessly in two languages, the horse eyeing the Mexican woman as she waved her hand to emphasize what she was saying.

"*Panchita, no es necesario esto! Alejandro lo puede.* He can ride like a monkey, and if he has to ride all night, it won't matter to him!" Alejandro was Josefina's grandson, only fourteen.

"Alejandro has to work on the big rock, Josefina. I can ride like a monkey, too, and I'm taking all I need to stay overnight. *Oiga!* if anyone comes past on the way to town, ask him to bring me some black powder — *no se cuanto, pero* — maybe five pounds, *que piensas?*"

"*No se, Panchita.* But there are lions out there. You must take a rifle!"

"All right — bring me his carbine, *la chiquita.*"

But when she held the carbine in her hands, and Josefina was lacing the scabbard to the saddle, she looked at the weapon in doubt. Like everything else Rip owned, the carbine was shamelessly decorated — engraved and inlaid, the scabbard hand-carved and dyed yellow, green, and red. Rip would be furious when she caught him out, and when he was angry he drank; when he was drunk he tried to drag her to bed, and she would have none of it any more. They were finished.

Could she trust herself with a gun? If she actually had to fight him off, would she shoot?

Yet it was true that there were mountain lions in those canyons a half day's ride west, and, more to the point, smugglers and wandering cow thieves. Finally she checked the magazine, put a shell in the chamber, and set the gun on safety. She took a deep breath, reached down to squeeze the hand of the Mexican woman, and said, *"Adios, Josefina!"*

"Adios, Panchita! Que te vayas bien!"

The previous night, the minute she laid eyes on the treasure map in Rip's boot, she had finally realized what he was up to: digging for the famous treasure of the Jesuits, like an army of men before him!

Ever since they were married, he had made frequent trips into Sonora to buy cattle, leaving her for months at a time to run the whole show, with nothing for help and protection but a Mexican woman and a boy too young to raise a mustache.

But the few cattle Rip brought home were sorry-looking critters. Once he had brought a leather bag with a couple of hundred silver pesos in it, which he admitted he had won on a bet of some kind. It was about as close as he had come to earning any money in all the time they had been married. The ranch was going downhill and they owed every innocent merchant who would trust Rip.

But what could you expect of a man you met in a graveyard and married a month later? Marrying any man named Rip had to be the act of a crazy woman. But she had been half insane with grief, visiting the churchyard everyday to sit on a camp stool and commune with Papa, reading him the poems he loved and keeping wildflowers in a jar on his grave.

And now, at last, she understood that she had leapt from the frying pan into the fire, like a lot of women before her. For Richard Parrish was a gambler, a part-time drunkard like his uncle, a skirt chaser, and a trifler. Her father could have told her — anyone could have. All the clues were there. His preposterous behavior in the graveyard! She simply had hypnotized herself into thinking he was heaven-sent. She had been in a half-mad condition. . . .

A number of other people had come and gone that day, two years ago, a few of them Mexican, more of them Anglo. Some of the Mexican people brought flowers, but most of them were uneasy in the Protestant cemetery, and they lit candles for him in their own church instead. *El Doctor Weemgard* had understood the Mexican people and their language, having practiced during winters in Sonora and summers in Nogales, after the desert got too hot. But of the gringos, only she brought flowers to the grave of Dr. John Wingard, who had delivered babies in this town and kept a lot of people out of this very graveyard. No one else came to pay his respects; not one hypocritical, Bible-quoting person!

Then one day a tall, high-shouldered man she had never seen before showed up carrying flowers. He wore a fringed leather coat and dark gray pants, a teal-blue Stetson with a silver band, fancy boots, and elaborately engraved spurs. His dark hair was abundant, with a few threads of gray, and his jawline beard and down-curving mustache made her think of Tennyson, one of Papa's favorite poets. His spurs clinked as he walked down the aisle to another new grave. Surreptitiously, Frances watched him stop at a weedy plot marked only with a small galvanized iron stake and a card behind glass. He was an arresting figure and she could not keep her eyes off him. She caught her breath as he drew a pint bottle of whiskey from his coat pocket. It was still sealed, and he cracked the tax stamp, drew the cork with a squeal, and, after a lift of the bottle toward the grave, drank some of the whiskey. As though it were a part of a ceremony, he poured the rest of the liquor on the gritty earth.

Frances covered her mouth to keep from giggling. He was having a drink with his — with whoever it was!

Solemnly, then, he thrust half the flowers

he carried into the neck of the bottle. Frances was charmed. *Half!* What would he do with the rest? Take them home to his wife?

For a full minute she watched as, hat off, head bowed, he stood at the foot of the grave. Once he cleared his throat, and she heard him say, "*Adios,* Uncle Hum. Acey-deucey-dicey, you old varmint!" The grave was unmarked, but Frances knew it was that of a man named Humboldt Parrish, an occasional patient of her father's who had owned a little ranch up the Santa Cruz River road. He had died only weeks before her father. An enigmatic, free-spending man, an occasional drunkard, Hum Parrish had won the ranch in a poker game. So this man was his nephew.

Frances brought herself back to the business of grieving, closing her eyes and asking God to forgive the ungrateful citizens of Nogales, Arizona Territory, for faulting a doctor who had done nothing every other doctor in the nation had not done, which was to prescribe drugs that turned out to be habit-forming. Nor was the new drug law his fault.

Suddenly she sniffed an intriguing blend of bay rum, whiskey, and Mulford Violets in the air. When she opened her eyes, she saw that the stranger was standing beside her. He smiled, nodded, and reached for her hands to help her up. There was no question of refusing. She actually had the thought that God had sent him here to take Papa's place. He was a foot taller than she, and gazed down into her face with a warm smile. His eyes were blue, his nose long, and the mints he was chewing were somehow an important part of the picture of this intriguing stranger.

"If you don't mind, ma'am," he said, "I've heard a great deal about your father, and I'd like to pay my respects. May I place these flowers with your own?"

"I can imagine what you've heard!" Frances burst out. "In this town what could you hear but the most scandalous — I'm sorry, I can't help being resentful."

"I considered the source, Miss Wingard, and . . . it was something about a Viennese Wine?"

"The Viennese Doctor's Wine of Coca." Frances nodded. "Every doctor in the country had his own pet remedy, catarrh powders that were plain narcotics! Dover's Powder, Mrs. Winslow's Soothing Syrup, morphine sulphate — but don't you know they blamed Papa because he practiced in Hermosillo as well as here? They considered him ungrateful to his own race. The Viennese doctor was a psychologist, a Dr. Froyd, it's spelled F-r-e-u-d, who wrote articles in the literature on the benefits of regular use of cocaine. Ha!" she cried. "Benefits, my eye!"

"Where is this Hermosillo, Miss . . . is it Wingard?"

"Yes. Frances Wingard." Demurely, eyes downcast.

"Richard Parrish. A pleasure."

"Thank you. Why, Hermosillo is the capital of Sonora, and we lived there in the winters. Hardly anything but lizards can live there in the summer, and even they wore straw hats. The people there needed good doctors, too, and it was an interesting city — lots of European people. The oldest university in North America, by the way! And the miserable hypocrites take it out on me because my father sent me to college! Can you imagine?" Then she put her hands over her mouth. "I'm sorry! Have I embarrassed you? But you see, there's no American person I can talk to, and I . . ."

"I understand, I surely do," Richard Parrish said. "I saved a few posies for your father, Miss Frances, and I hope you won't mind if . . ."

He went to one knee and placed his flowers in the bowl with Frances's own.

"Why, aren't you nice, Mr. Parrish!" Frances said, her heart melting toward him. She bit her lip and turned her head away but failed

39

to keep from sobbing. Richard Parrish had put his arms around her and held her, patting her back and murmuring to her as though she were a child.

Barely a month later, Frances and Rip Parrish were married. Frances went to live on the ranch Rip had inherited from his Uncle Hum, the gambler, out of reach, at last, of the hypocritical tongues and puritanical eyes of the unappreciative townspeople of Nogales.

But now the dream become nightmare was over, and it was simply a question of informing him that she was leaving him, and wanted a little money for all the improvements she had made in the ranch, with what little cash her father had left her. And God forbid she should ever meet a man in a graveyard again!

Chapter Four

Henry found the boarding stable Ben Ambrose had recommended at the north end of the business district, a large tin-roofed adobe barn with a liver-medicine advertisement painted on the side. With a black iron bolt he rang a horseshoe hanging by the door, and then set to work unsaddling. In a moment a big shirtless man in bib overalls emerged. Ambrose had said his name was Budge Gorman. He wore a black Grand Army hat pulled so far down on his face that he had to tip his head back to see Henry, which caused his mouth, innocent of upper teeth, to gape. He had long, hairy arms and a face like a hound.

Henry made arangements for the horse.

He asked the stableman how to find Alice Gary's place, and the big simple man took a hoof pick and squatted down in the hard-packed dirt. With deep, rasping scratches, he drew a map.

"This here's Morley. Yonder's Sonoyta.

Walk straight up the hill and turn right. Top of the hill. You can't miss it. Try to buy that bracelet from Allie. I ain't never seen it off her wrist, and I swear to God it's too big for me!"

"How big is she?"

"Size of a sparrow!" The laugh from Budge's deep, hairy chest sounded like *hee, hee, hee!* About right for Allie.

The climb was steep. When Henry arrived, breathing deeply, a Mexican girl with a long shining braid but no English led him to a bedroom in the rear where his bags rested on the floor beside a cot with a white counterpane. She tried to explain something to him but finally giggled and went away.

The room was much more comfortable than he had expected, the walls covered with flocked cream-colored wallpaper, the high ceiling of stamped tin painted gray. There was a flowered porcelain fixture on one wall like nothing he had ever seen — a little china tank with a faucet, and a matching bowl below it. The brass bed was narrow, and near the window stood a small desk and a fragile chair. A bowl and pitcher reminded him to take his quinine, and he measured the dose into a water glass, filled it from a pitcher, and bolted it. The bitter taste almost curled his hair. Gasping, he made terrible faces at the mirror until he could get the cork out of a pint bottle of whiskey and down a slug. As always, he gasped. "Great snakes!"

Recovering, he brushed aside a glass-bead curtain and gazed down into the almost treeless bowl that held the town. The near hillside fell by terraces that held rows of small homes. At the bottom, one- and two-story business houses lined the north- and south-running streets. Water towers on stilts rose above the railroad station.

The far hillside appeared to be covered with cave dwellings, pole sheds, hovels, and privies. Lines of wash flapped in the breeze. He saw Spanish bayonet and a few mesquite, but nothing a respectable horticulturist would honestly call a tree.

Downtown, the streets ran capriciously, meeting to form wedgelike corners two fat people could hardly stand on. It would be a surveyor's nightmare, the only level land seeming to be where the railroad tracks lay like a basking snake between the hills. Yet, built though the town was of tin roofs and dirt, and completely undecorated, he liked it — the foreign smells, the lusty honking of a burro somewhere, and the cool, clean, cell-like room he stood in. It was completely free of clutter — exactly the kind of room a man needed who had some serious thinking to do.

In fact, he realized, the room put him in mind of his little bedroom at Fort Bowie.

He studied himself in the mirror on the dresser. Was his skin a little more yellow? Definitely. Well, at least he had gotten this far without a spell of ague.

He stretched out on the white iron cot for his first real sleep in days, and sank into oblivion. . . .

When he opened his eyes, the light in the room had faded. He lay still, enjoying the sounds of children's voices calling in Spanish. He sniffed something that smelled like apple pie. An idea had come to him as he slept: that since Rip's Uncle Hum was buried here, Rip's widow probably would have had him buried in the same cemetery, if he were dead. Tomorrow he would talk to the county recorder, but this afternoon he could check the cemetery, if it was not too far away.

He hadn't had time to think about Manion's telegram. What did "advise caution" mean, exactly? At least it would be the part of wisdom to tell no one what he was doing here.

He found the bathroom, spruced up, and walked down a hall to a kitchen. A small, aproned woman was standing at a worktable with her back to him. He tapped on the doorjamb, and she turned, her hands white with flour.

"Well, Mr. Logan!" she said. "Did you have a nice rest?" She was dark-haired and pretty, and he spotted at once the huge gold bracelet on her left wrist, massive enough for a mule skinner.

"I slept like a dead man," Henry said. "I need to ask about board, Mrs. Gary."

She told him he could call her Allie, that room and board was fifteen dollars a month or five dollars a week, and that sheets were changed weekly. Henry paid a month's board, using one of his gold pieces. She gave him some silver coins for change.

"We use Mexican pesos here," she said. "They go for fifty cents." Henry liked the big cold coins' honest heft on his palm, their slick feel and the fierce eagle on a cactus, a rattlesnake in its beak; he clinked them on his hand a couple of times before dropping them in his pocket.

"I have a question, Allie. Whereabouts would I find a cemetery?"

She tried to suppress her amusement but giggled. "Oh, now you don't look *that* bad," she said.

"I had malaria," Henry said. "A friend thought I might feel better here, so —"

"You will, Henry, you surely will! I like to

died in San Franciso — the damp. I had bronchitis. Here, I'm healthy as a horse. Will you be looking for work?"

"Depends on how I feel. First off, though, I'm looking for —"

"A cemetery. Well, if you walk south, you'll soon be on Cemetery Hill. There's also a lot of little houses where retired soldiers from Fort Huachuca have settled. And a bigger one where General Stockard and his wife, Emily, live. She's going senile, poor thing. Tomorrow you'll have time to visit the other cemeteries, if you're a mind. Dinner's at six and I ring the triangle on the porch. That's funny," she said. "Most people want to see where the Yaquis burned the buildings, or where the Maid of Caborca was captured. You must have a relative or friend . . . ?"

Henry recited what John Manion had told him. "I'm trying to help a lawyer friend in Kansas City. A client of his passed away a while back, and there was a small fund for perpetual care. I promised I'd make sure —"

Allie giggled. "Surely they didn't send you to Arizona to count weeds on a grave?"

"Alice" — Henry chuckled — "there is no fooling you. The truth is, I'm with the Kansas City zoo, and I'm collecting roadrunners. They told me they're thick in cemeteries."

He heard her laughing as he went down the hall.

The houses on the west side of the street stood several feet higher than those on Allie's side, all of them built of adobe, with peaked roofs and galleries running all around them like steamboats. On the walk to the cemetery, Henry saw some flowers growing by the road, and he picked a few lupines and Indian paintbrush for Humboldt Parrish's grave. Finally he came to the cemetery, a small, tilted, bedraggled half acre inside a rusty barbed-wire fence. Here and there Spanish bayonet and scrub oak grew from the caliche soil. A black buggy stood near a wrought-iron gate, and a gray horse, stone-anchored, browsed on the yellow weeds. The rig had a funereal look, as though plumes should stand in the whip sockets. But what was fixed on the nigh side, he saw, was a rifle in a scabbard. He leaned down to study it, and pursed his lips.

Nice! Excellent piece of the gun maker's art. The gun stock was of carved rosewood; the barrel, walls, and magazine of nickel steel. Looked like a Hotchkiss, what he could see of it, a gun Winchester had tried to sell the Army, so that a few officers got them. The weapon very much resembled his father's carbine — the one that had disappeared in the raid, or been burned and melted down totally. He eased it halfway from the scabbard and confirmed that it was the same model, then looked for the fortunate owner.

There he was — *she* was! — sitting by a grave, reading a book as big as a Bible. He conjectured: Would it be polite to ask a lady in a cemetery where she had come by a weapon? (And, if he got past this hurdle, would she like to trade for a newer gun that held more cartridges?)

Nothing ventured, he decided.

A rusty hinge gave an iron squall as he opened the gate. The mourner, a young woman, sat on a folding stool on the central aisle; she did not look up, but as he started toward her he came to a shocked halt. Though he saw her face in profile, he was certain it was the woman in the wedding picture! She had the same arch way of holding her head; even the braid brought forward across one shoulder was that of the woman in the photograph. She wore a white shirtwaist with a high collar and a full tan skirt; a little straw hat lay on the ground beside her.

Holding his breath, he studied his cards.

As of the time Manion got her wire, Frances Parrish's husband was missing.

Had he been found — and buried — in the few days since?

No, for the grave had settled completely.

He decided there was one person could give him all the information he needed. The Widow Parrish.

As yet she had not seen him. She was writing furiously on one of those officers' field desks. He saw her suddenly thrust her fingers into her hair, stare at her paper, seeming distracted — then, with a shake of her head, dip her pen and scribble on. What a fine, theatrical gesture, perfect for so vital-looking a woman as the doctor's daughter. He sensed, however, that she would not appreciate being interrupted at her work.

So: He would stroll past, carrying his blue-and-red nosegay, and steal a glance at the marker. If not Rip's grave, then whose? He would walk on, then, and find Hum Parrish's grave. When she appeared to be finished with whatever she was writing, he could introduce himself.

Chapter Five

In the late afternoon, Frances Parrish sat on a camp stool beside her father's grave, his old field desk on her lap, meticulously setting down the story of her husband's death.

Or was he dead? She had never seen his body, but there had been such a welter of blood on the ground that she presumed he had been shot and his body dragged away. Yet she had never seen him after that night. And just as she was beginning to hope that people would decide that Rip had wandered on, a trifler like him, and forget about him, a letter appeared at the post office that shocked her out of her wits.

The lawyer in Kansas City warned Rip that unless he heard from him promptly, the trust checks would cease.

And then yesterday a telegram was waiting for her when she arrived in town, informing her that a gunman named Henry Logan would arrive shortly to make inquiries. Now her anxiety exploded into panic.

A gunman! *Why,* in heaven's name? Did he think she was some wild gun-toting woman who had killed her husband and would kill again? But whatever the man called himself, his first move would certainly be to alert the county sheriff to the situation at Spider Ranch. She imagined herself sitting across a desk from George Bannock, that colossal, poky man with the bitter little eyes like rivet heads, and the grisly whisper of a voice. And he, too, had his own reason for hating her father, for Dr. Wingard had cut the deadly growth off his larynx and turned him into the croaking giant they called Whispering George.

Why haven't you (something, something, something), Miz Frances? he would begin.

I'm sorry, Sheriff — I didn't catch all of that.

Blame your father for that, ma'am. They used to call me Big George Bannock. Now it's Whispering George. I said, why haven't you reported your husband missing?

Because I was afraid I might be accused of Rip's murder. And he takes off like this so often. So you see, Sheriff, I'm not even sure he's dead. . . .

Weren't you ever going to report him missing, Miz Frances? The grisly death's-head voice barely comprehensible. She had to hold her breath to make out the words, but the glint of his eyes was always eloquent.

Well, I thought I'd wait a spell, she would say offhandedly. *Richard might still come back . . .*

How long a spell were you thinking of, ma'am? (Here he would cough, making the most of his disability.)

Oh — I suppose a year or so.

A year, Miz Frances? Leaning toward her like a Tower of Pisa about to bury her in bricks.

Yes, sir. Mas o menos.

You'd better get yourself a lawyer, dear lady.

So she decided to talk to that lawyer Rip's Uncle Hum had used — Ira Gustetter. He was a disgusting creature, and his wife had cut Frances on the street. But since he was a pariah, too, some common feeling might grow between them.

She had driven in the previous night and stayed with a Mexican family she knew in the other Nogales. Then she learned this morning that Gustetter was ill — ill, indeed! drunk or hung over — and she would have to stay overnight again. Just as well — she really ought to set down everything before trying to tell anyone. Even the fact that it had rained the day she rode out there might be important — it was why she had arrived at the worst possible time, at sundown, with Rip getting drunk.

So she put this down.

I was sure that my husband was camped at Spanish Church, on our ranch, so I left early that morning, August 14, to try to find him. I wanted to be early enough, if possible, that I could get back home the same evening. . . .

But a hard summer storm made her late in arriving at the spot. She had to stay out of the canyons and on the hillsides, which were slow going. At last, sunburned and tired, she rode out onto a bench over-looking a wash far back in the maze of canyons and volcanic hills on the western edge of the ranch. The ruins of a small adobe church spread over part of the bench. She could see right through the fabled Spanish Church, its south wall having melted into a berm. The structure was roof-less, and its doors had been taken away long since. Weeds and shrubs sprouted from the tops of the broken mud-brick walls.

Below her in the wash, a shallow creek lapped against a volcanic cliff. Downstream a few hundred feet, the cliff split open and a side canyon joined the main one. In this delta there was a tiny meadow with a little grass and some hackberry trees and oaks, but mostly it had been taken over by brush. A trail continued up this side canyon to end abruptly a half mile south in a box canyon with steep, colorful stone cliffs. A stone fence had been erected across the mouth of the side canyon, making it a perfect holding place when cattle were being worked.

Against the left-hand wall of this natural pen stood a rock house, out of sight from where she was. Near the cabin was the entrance to the so-called fabulous Padres Mine with its pile of rubble. ("Dig here," it said on the map!) She could see no one but smelled wood smoke and green chilis. A Mexican was cooking his supper down there — not Rip, for all he could cook was bacon and beans. There was simply no doubt that someone, possibly a cattle thief or smuggler, was going to have green chilis, fried and skinned in an iron skillet and probably served with melted goat cheese, plus badly scorched tortillas; along with, let's see — refried beans and *salsa picante*. Her nose, brought up on Mexican smells, read the aromas like items on a restaurant menu.

Frances dismounted and went toward the church, carrying Rip's carbine. She did not intend to be taken by surprise by whoever was camped down there. Two imposing but crumbling pilasters of rock and mud marked the church entrance. Set into one was an illegible sandstone plaque with a cross still visible in it. Looking right and left, she picked her way through the shell to the cemetery at the rear. Here, within a rectangle of stones laid without mortar to form a wall were aisles of graves, most of them slightly sunken, like cheeks where teeth were missing; they were unmarked, or commemorated only by rusty iron crosses. A few lichened stone crosses remained, and there were the rotten shreds of wooden markers. With the gun off-safety, Frances picked her way through the cemetery to a stone wall beyond which a trail led to a wash. There was a small orchard here with a depressing crop of blighted fruit. She stood among the gnarled fruit trees while she studied the canyon below.

Suddenly a banjo began a nasal twanging. A man's voice embarked on a song Frances knew well, *"Amor y Lágrimas."* She smirked. She had tried to teach the song to Rip, playing along on her mandolin. But he considered Spanish an inferior language, and his banjo playing made her shudder. Smelling the chilis again, she thought, *Well, well, Rip Parrish! And when did we learn how to skin green chilis, hmm?*

She went back for her horse and rode down the trail to the wash.

At the near edge of the stream, where it was less than a foot deep, the horse lowered its head and commenced noisily sucking up water and pawing at the stones in it. At the same time a dog somewhere in the camp began an uproar, and she could see it tearing through the camp now, toward the wash. The camp, forty or fify feet beyond the sand-bars, occupied slightly raised ground. A fire burned in a hole. The rock house was against the cliff, off to the left. A man sat by the fire, on a stump, the banjo on his lap. He was not playing now, merely plucking a random note now and then as he tried to see who was coming. She could not see the color of his roll-brim hat, but it was exactly the shape of her husband's high-crowned, teal-blue sombrero and had its wide-curled brim.

Roaring like a whole pack of hounds, the dog came splashing through the shallow stream, and she had to control the horse. But the dog, some kind of Australian sheepdog Rip had picked up, recognized her and the horse and ceased its barking. Sitting her horse, Frances ran a quick score of what she was up against. The camp was no overnight affair. A canvas food-safe hung from the branch of a tree; there was a little wood-pile of *manzanita* roots and some tools, and a dishpan and wash-tub hung against the wall of the cabin.

Frances rode on across the creek to the south bank and the man came to his feet and watched her approach. He wore a miner's blue chambray shirt, work pants, and heavy shoes, and it was Rip Parrish. Frances dismounted in silence, neither of them uttering a syllable. Without speaking, she loosened the cinches of her saddle, then went up and looked into his face. The firelight revealed that he was tired and out of sorts. He was unshaven, his jawline beard and drooping mustache were shabby, and his long black hair looked ragged.

"How she goin', Panchita?" Rip said, picking up a dusty wine bottle.

"Not very well, Rip," Frances said.

"Don't call me Reep," he said, mimicking her. "My name's Rip."

"I wouldn't brag about it. Are you going to let those chilis burn to ash?"

"Don't you be worrying' about my dinner, Frances," Rip said. "And don't be figuring to stay. I don't encourage women henpecking after me."

"Is this what you call buying cattle in Sonora?" Frances said. She pulled the pin out of her hat, dropped the hat on a boulder, and shook her hair out. And waited, smirking.

Rip had another pull of wine. "Is that a bit of fire I see in your flashing eyes?" he said.

"More likely tears. We've got some serious

talking to do. Would you like to go first?"

"First and last, Panchita. I have put up with your namby-pamby moralizing bullshit as long as I mean to. I'm going to say this once only. I have just come back from Sonora, broke and tired and needing none of your womanly carping and mincing around. I intend —"

"Oh, I don't propose to mince!" Frances cut in, rage making her breathless. "That's over. Do you know the meaning of that song you were singing, 'Amor y Lágrimas'? It means 'Love and Tears,' and you've given me a year and a half of *lágrimas* and mighty little *amor*, and I'm having no more of it, Rip Parrish."

"Reep! Reep! My name ain't Reep." Rip smirked. "Can't you even speak English?"

Her accent was a sore point. People in Nogales snickered at it, too. Her eyes flashed, but she ignored his sarcasm.

"Don't you realize there are idiots like you all over this border digging for the so-called 'Treasure of the Padres'? Not to mention the lost mines, the lost Army gold, the lost thees, the lost that? Well, *Reep*, eet's going to be the lost Spider Ranch een a few more months!"

"You might be surprised, woman."

Frances pressed the back of her band to her brow. She was just about finished. Her hand

58

dropped wearily and she exclaimed, "Oh, I do hope you'll surprise me! What have you found? A broken seventeenth-century teacup in the popular Sears, Roebuck pattern?"

Rip grinned and offered the wine bottle. "Like your spunk, Panchita. Have a snort — for the road. . . ."

With scorn she looked him over, head to foot, but with the clear vision of a stranger this time. When he was on display, like a blooded horse, he could be *muy caballero*, handsome and courtly. But the lips that looked as sensitive as a poet's were more given to uttering the most insensitive things. She waved the bottle away.

"Why did you speak to me that day in the cemetery?"

"That's easy. I needed a new woman for my new ranch, along with my new clothes. Part of the outfit."

"So it had nothing to do with respect for Papa, as you told me? Putting flowers on his grave was just like, like, bringing me a bottle of perfume?"

"Tears your mind up, don't it?" Rip grinned.

"'He will hold thee, when his passion shall have spent its novel force, / Something better than his dog, a little dearer than his horse.' Papa told me about that poem of Tennyson's," said Frances. "And now at last I understand it."

Rip gulped the mouthful of wine he had just taken and gave an angry roar. "Papa, Papa, Papa! I am so fed up hearing about that old horse-doctor of a *papa*, I could puke! I tell you, woman, it's like living with a ghost in the house!"

Frances's mouth trembled in hurt. "He was the finest doctor this country ever saw," she said. "The most compassionate and the most tireless."

Rip stabbed a finger in her face, making her tilt her head back. "Your famous papa! Famous for leaving a town full of dope fiends!" He laughed.

Frances had to clear her throat before she could speak. "He did just exactly what all the other doctors in this nation did, and you know it and they know it. As for Nogales doctors — Tracy or Halleck or Sherwood or Fish — they all put opium in their soothing syrups and tonics, and some used morphine sulphate. Catarrh powders, Mrs. Winslow's — it had morphine, for heaven's sake, and recommended for children!"

Rip moved toward her, his smile taunting and warning. Frances backed away. "Well, then, tell me, Miz Parrish — why *do* they only blame Papa?"

Frances struck at his face, and he leaned back, saying, "My, my!"

"They blamed him because he practiced in the capital of Sonora in the winters and here in the summer. I suppose they felt it was disloyal to them — but he practiced there first when we came from the East for Mama's health. He treated the governor's family, and all the most important people in Hermosillo, as well as —"

Rip blew a hooting note across the neck of the wine bottle and slugged down a mouthful. "Maybe he was a little too important — to you, that is. . . ."

"What do you mean?" Haughtily.

"You may be a married woman, Frances, but in your heart you're still an old maid, and always will be. You're the unnatural bride of that old horse-doctor of a father."

With hurt and rage she stared at him. Rip tickled her chin. Frances slapped his hand away.

"Know something, though?" Rip said. "The most important woman I ever had in my bed was you. That's a fact, Panchita. Was fornication one of your subjects at . . . where was it, Swarthmore?"

"Stevens," Frances said, snatching up the carbine and thrusting it against his chest as he put his hands on her shoulders. Rip backed off, startled. The dog squared off to Frances and, snarling, showed its fangs. But Rip kicked at the animal and it slunk away.

"Jesus Christ, Frances!" He gasped. "Don't you know yet when I'm funning you?"

Frances rattled the bolt of the carbine. "I'm not funning you, Reep Parrish," she said. "I'm warning you that you've laid a hand on me for the last time. I'm going back to the ranch now, and I'll be gone when you come home."

"Then let's shake hands on it," Rip said. "It's over and done with. Adios, and don't come back."

Frances heard a door hinge creak. Rip turned his head and called sharply: "Hey! What did I tell you?" In the dusk she saw a woman wearing a black rebozo come from the cabin. She carried a shawl with its corners drawn up to make a sack. Smiling shyly, she came to where she could speak to Frances. She was Mexican, young and pretty, with the Oriental features of Southern Mexico.

"Please say to him I am sorry. I go back now."

Rip rubbed his face with his palms. He seemed tired and frustrated. "What's she say?" he asked Frances.

"She's leaving. I'm sorry, too," Frances said to the woman. "I didn't know he had company. I'm his wife. You don't need to leave. I'm leaving, myself."

"No, señora, excuse me, I must go. Adios, Reep."

Frances felt sorry for the woman, probably a prostitute from Nogales or Oro Blanco. Swinging the laden shawl onto her back, she smiled at Frances and said, "The *rellenos* are burning, señora. Adios."

"Adios, señorita. What is your name?"

"*Cata-Catalina Cachora, a su servicio.*"

"*Mucho placer,*" Frances murmured.

The woman hurried off into the shadows, Rip's dog trotting with her. A few moments later Frances heard a burro's quick little hooves clattering up the trail. Then the carbine was suddenly torn from her hands, and Rip's palm slapped her cheek. He lunged, got his arms around her, and picked her up. He smelled of sweat, wine, and sulfur. (Sulfur? she thought. Is he smelting ore out here?) Laughing, ripping her shirtwaist open and pretending to snap at her breast, he carried her toward the cabin like a vandal's bride. Fiercely she struggled to scratch his face, to bite his neck, but he roared with laughter and locked her arms to her sides.

She stopped struggling and tried to think. Papa had told her something about an acutely sensitive part of a man's anatomy; that almost anything that happened to it, if it was forceful enough, was enough to "unman" him, as the saying went. When he reacted to her going limp by releasing her wrist, she reached down and squeezed and twisted with all her strength. Rip howled and sank to his knees, letting Frances sprawl on the ground. As she crawled away, he lay doubled up on the ground, gasping and moaning.

She looked around, sobbing in desperation. Even if she could reach her horse, the cinch was loosened and the saddle would turn under her; and, anyway, Rip's big Morgan could easily outrun the mare. She looked for the carbine, but he had slung it into the brush. She heard him swearing as he got to his feet. As he reached for her, she screamed, and the pure, instinctive, nerve-racking female sound startled him, giving her an instant to run for the cabin.

The small room was feebly illuminated by a candle in a cranberry votive glass before a *santo* on a table. The door was made from hewn poles. With all her strength she banged it closed and swung the bar into the wooden keeper. An instant later Rip crashed against it.

"Open the goddamn door!" he bawled. "I'm going to teach you that when I say frog, you better jump next time! I'm going to whip your backside raw, woman!"

He attacked the door with his fists, his shoulder, a rock; then, grunting curses, he tramped away. *Oh, my God, Frances,* she thought, *he will murder you after he rapes you.* She knelt before the shrine. Although she was a badly failed Catholic, she prayed. Then, opening her eyes as she heard Rip outside the door again, she saw something hanging behind the bed on which she was about to be sacrificed, like an Aztec maiden. She whispered,

"Dios Mío, te doy gracias! Gracias, Señor!"

She seized the holstered gun hanging from a nail and pulled out Rip's ornately engraved Colt. It was obviously loaded, since she could scarcely raise it to point it. Breathing like a frightened horse, she sat on the bed and waited, occupying herself in pulling the hammer back. As the thing went on full cock, it made a harsh sound like the snapping of an iguana's jaws.

Rip's boots came tramping back, the dog barking as it ran alongside him. "This ain't even legal!" he shouted. "What about my husbandly rights? Open this door or I'll chop my way in!"

"Leave me alone, Rip! I warn you!"

An ax or sledge struck the door. Dust flew. Another blow opened a wide crack from top to bottom. Frances sat on the bed and raised the revolver with both hands. She took a wavering aim at a knot high in the door, too high to hit him but close enough to scare him. She closed her eyes and squeezed the trigger.

The world exploded with a blinding flash and a roar. A wind struck her face. After the orange flash faded, she could see nothing whatsoever. Absolutely deaf and blind, shocked by the colossal explosion, she sat on the bed wondering whether she had blinded herself. At last she realized the concussion must have blown the candle out.

She sat there waiting. She heard nothing from outside but recognized that she probably could not have heard a cannon shot. What was Rip doing out there in the darkness?

She lay back on the bed to wait for what should come next, which might be her own death. Then, so relieved that she began to cry, she heard Rip playing the banjo and singing. With the relief came exhaustion; she let herself fall back on the cot, to lie with ringing ears in a sort of coma. She dreamed that Rip came to the door and said, "This is a plate of food, Panchita. I'll be over at the fire. If you need anything, just call. I won't fuss with you anymore. I'm truly sorry."

But it was not a dream, she fathomed at last. What kind of creature is this, she thought, who says and does cruel things when he's sober, and kind things when he's drunk?

When she heard him picking and singing again, yawning and getting sleepier by the minute, she sneaked the plate of food into the cabin. It was cold and greasy, of course, but eased out some of her tension and raised her spirits. After eating, she lay down again. She dared not unbar the door, which seemed to make her a prisoner and him her jailer.

I suppose, she thought, *what I am doing is illegally denying my husband his marital rights.* Remembering the cruel thing he had said about her father fixation, she comprehended at last that he was right: She might never be able to love a man fully, since no man could ever take Papa's place in her life. Yet some man must, or she was doomed to be an old maid, at least in her heart.

Crying softly, she curled up on the cot and slept.

Frances was about to write the final page of her story when she realized that the young auburn-haired man with the liverish complexion was standing at the foot of the grave, only a few feet away! Despite his smile, in his black frock coat and trousers he looked like Death's dark angel come for someone in the cemetery, possibly herself.

She closed the writing tablet quickly and

banged the desk closed, then shot him a single angry glance and prepared to leave, hoping he would be intimidated and go away. But he remained, and she heard him ask, most respectfully: "Excuse me, ma'am — aren't you Mrs. Parrish? I knew you from your wedding picture. I'm Henry Logan, from Kansas City, a friend of John Manion's. I don't mean to intrude, but we really do have to talk."

Chapter Six

The woman in the cemetery turned in surprise to stare at him, her face pale. He had studied that face so many times that every feature was familiar, as though he had known her for years. But the archness he had seen in it was missing — in fact, now that he was noticing the flared nostrils and quick breathing, what he saw was fright.

"I'm sorry?" she said. "My wedding picture? I don't understand."

"I'm Henry Logan. Your husband sent the picture to my attorney friend," Henry said. He had already checked the marker and found that two names were carved into it, neither of them Richard Parrish's.

ELIZABETH MOTLEY WINGARD. WILLIAM MAKEPEACE WINGARD.

He remembered that she was a Wingard — that the bride's name on the photograph had been inscribed "Frances Wingard Parrish."

Again she thrust her fingers into her hair, distractedly, as though a bee had lodged there.

"Well, I can't talk to you now! I have to see my attorney before I can talk to anyone. And please don't leave the flowers!" she exclaimed, brushing him away as he went to one knee to place them in the vase on the grave. "Put them . . . on his uncle's grave." Her hand continued to wave him off like a beggar.

But Henry smiled and went on arranging the wildflowers. "Oh, my," he said. "I knew there was fire behind that face. Now, I don't know who you think I am, but I'm here to help you, not make trouble for you."

"Ha!" she cried. "Well, I don't need a gunman's help!"

Henry looked up from the flowers. Then he laughed. "A gunman? I'm not a gunman, Mrs. Parrish. Where did you get that notion?"

She extended her arm down the hill toward the depot. "The telegram. It came yesterday. That man in Kansas City, he said for my husband to extend all . . . courtesies or something, to a gunman named Logan, who was going to ask some questions."

Henry stood up. "That's rich. I'm a gun-*smith*, which has nothing to do with my being here, anyway."

Frances said, "Oh, that idiotic telegrapher! You want to know where my husband is, is that it?" She definitely had a faint accent — another intriguing element in her, like a peekaboo blouse promising hidden charms.

"That's it," Henry said. "I simply need to find and talk to Richard."

The uptilted blue eyes mocked him. "So do a few other people, Mr. Logan, including a number of merchants and his wife."

"He's missing, then?"

"To put it . . . prudently. . . ."

Henry could not take his eyes off her, and his persistent gaze finally drove hers down. She began readying her desk, book, and chair to carry to the buggy.

"Mr. Logan," she said, "I'll talk to you to-morrow. I'm going back to the ranch pretty early — it's a long drive — but I'll talk to you first. Where are you staying?"

He told her. The intent blue eyes scrutinized his face. "What are you doing for your jaundice?" she asked suddenly.

"What? Taking quinine." He shrugged. "Know of anything better?"

"That's basic, of course. But my father had another remedy that is excellent for the liver. Unfortunately I didn't bring any into town with me. He was a doctor," she explained.

"So your husband wrote. He gave Manion the impression that your father was highly re-garded as a healer."

"Ho, ho, ho! Not in this town!" Frances

said scoffingly. "What else did he say about Papa?"

"That he took care of a lot of important people — a governor, French geologists, and the like."

"That was in Hermosillo, Mr. Logan — in Sonora, Mexico. He practiced there in the winters. It gets hot enough to addle a pit viper's brains in the summer, so we'd come up here. Well, I'm glad Rip had something good to say about him. . . ."

"Here, I'll carry those," Henry said. She was trying to pick up the desk and chair at the same time with the book under one arm.

He loaded them into the buggy for her, placed the stone anchor on the floorboard, and helped her up. He checked the harness for her, said, "All set!" and then remembered the carbine. "May I look at this?"

"Certainly. It was — it's my husband's."

Henry drew the weapon, clicked his heels and came to attention, then did his little manual of arms routine, and Frances laughed as he finished with a mock shot into the air.

" 'Ease!" Then he relaxed and looked the rifle over. "It's been well taken care of," he commented.

"Yes . . ." A quick sidelong look.

"I'd like to fire it sometime."

"Certainly. Mr. Logan, if you like, you may ride out to Spider Ranch with me tomorrow morning. I'll tell you everything I know, which may be less exciting than what you might hear from some others in this town but which happens to be true. There are some papers of my husband's . . . things like that."

"That would be bully, as my commanding officer used to say."

She raised her brows. "Colonel Roosevelt?"

"Teddy, himself. He scratched out a foreword to a little Army manual I wrote in Cuba. So many of these city boys were accidentally shooting themselves — totally mystified by guns. I have some copies at Allie's."

"How interesting! I'd love to read it. What did you call it?"

"*The Law of the Gun.* Too Fred Fearnot?"

She smiled. "Well, I don't think boy recruits would jump at *Some Thoughts on Firearms.* No — bully for you, Henry!"

He grinned. "Manion wrote something, too — just for you. If Richard is deceased, these papers will attest that you are the widow, and, ah, the trust would then be transferred to you as your sole and separate property. . . . If it's desertion, well . . ."

"Oh, that's nice. Although the problems are really just . . ." She raised and dropped her hands. "It's hopeless!"

"Nothing is hopeless, Mrs. Parrish. We'll tackle the problems tomorrow. One at a time. All right?"

"Thank you. I'm sorry we had to meet in a cemetery, because that's where I met Rip, and what a terrible mistake that was! I'll come to Alice's at, mmm, nine o'clock?"

"Fine. I've got to buy some Arizona clothes — I look like an undertaker in this outfit. It goes back to before I met that Cuban mosquito."

"Yes, you'll need jeans and a strong shirt. Your Army boots will be fine for the canyon ride. A brush-popper jacket, maybe."

"The canyon ride," Henry said, closing one eye.

"The ride to the place I'm going to show you. It's way out in the canyons. . . ."

Driving back, she had nothing to say until, as he went toward the porch, she called after him: "Mr. Logan? As a doctor's daughter, I'd advise you to take no spirits at all. None — including beer."

"I'll remember. Thank you."

She gave him a wan smile, clucked up her funereal gray horse, and he knew his goose was cooked.

He was in love with this woman. Whatever she might have done with her husband. Whatever surprises might lie below the quiet beauty of her face. Come what may, he was in love with Frances Wingard Parrish. And, God forgive him, he hoped her husband was dead.

Chapter Seven

Using an overturned dresser for a desk, Henry scribbled a message for John Manion: "Interesting error by telegrapher: Gunman for gunsmith. Visiting ranch tomorrow."

Then, tormented by the supper smells, he hurried to wash up, using the nice flowered porcelain washbowl attached to the wall. He walked down the hall to the dining room and glanced inside. He saw that Alice Gary set a nice table. On a clean white cloth rested cut-glass cruets for vinegar and oil, silver napkin rings, even a decanter of red wine and cut-glass goblets. As Henry stood behind his chair, Allie introduced the other boarders.

"Miss Leisure? Arthur B. Cleveland?" her hand pointing, huge golden eagle flashing on her wrist. "This is Mr. Henry Logan, from Kansas City."

At Henry's left sat a very old lady in a black dress with jet buttons. She sat on a pillow that enabled her to reach the table. Tiny, frail as a thistle, she looked as though a puff of wind would blow her away. She offered a yellow-toothed smile and a brittle hand protected by a lace mitt.

"So nice to meet you, Henruh," she said in a soft accent.

"Pleased to meet you, ma'am."

"What church d'y'all go to?" Miss Leisure asked.

"Well . . . I haven't gotten settled as yet, but —"

Sensing that he might be a backslider, Allie hastily introduced the old man, also in black and nearly as old as Miss Leisure. He was a retired bookkeeper from Portland who had come here for his asthma. He had a long skinny neck, a small head, and an oversize beak, and made Henry think of a baby eagle. His watery eyes were red-rimmed under bald brows.

Everyone seemed to have wine at his place, so Henry poured himself a couple of fingers — remembered what Frances had said about alcohol and hesitated — but decided a good time to start self-denial would be tomorrow, after a night's sleep.

It seemed to him, as serving dishes were passed, that they all stole looks at him as though he were a magician and they didn't want to miss a move — that his hand might be quicker than their eyes. Allie seemed troubled. He still heard her laughter as he had left, but now she was quiet and sober.

Henry finally asked her: "Anything wrong, Allie? Was my money counterfeit?"

"No, Henry. I'm just thoughtful."

"Uh-huh. Well, penny for your thoughts," he said.

"Pshaw. I'm not sure you're going to like the story the *Globe* ran on you tonight. At least I don't. . . ."

The old man eagerly thrust a folded newspaper at him. "God's Gunman!"

"*What?*"

Henry opened the paper, saw the banner line, NOTED GUNMAN IN TOWN TO DRAW BEAD ON KILLER OF MISSING MAN. He looked out the window. "My God," he muttered. "Is this man — what's-his-name, Ambrose? — insane?"

Allie thumped her brow with the heel of her hand. "He's a snake," she said. "But, Henry! I didn't pry, but I couldn't help seeing the guns in your luggage — and I have to say that, that if you plan anything —"

"Let me read this first. . . ."

"God made me a sharpshooter," Henry Logan told the *Globe* this morning, "and Colonel Roosevelt recognized my unusual gift and made me a sniper in his regiment. Shooting ability like mine is given to few men, and I am one of the fortunate. I can take the ash off a mosquito's cigarette at a hundred yards. I lost count of how many Spanish soldiers I drilled. But gunman? Well, I wouldn't say that. . . ."

Henry raised his eyes from the paper, gazed through a window down upon the business district. Streetlights were coming on, haloed by dust. He whistled and resumed reading.

Logan, fronting for a Kansas City attorney, is in Nogales to investigate the disappearance last year of Richard I. "Rip" Parrish, owner of the Spider Ranch north of town.

Friends of Parrish have long feared that his cattle-buying trip to Sonora ended in tragedy. The popular young man has not been seen or heard from in approximately eight months.

Parrish's wife, Frances Wingard Parrish, daughter of the controversial physician, William Makepeace Wingard, has so far not reported him missing. An official investigation of his mysterious disappearance must await such an action on her part, or a decision on the part of County Sheriff G. H. "Whispering George" Bannock, not yet forthcoming, to look into the matter. Certainly there appear to be grounds for an assumption of foul play.

Asked whether his rare shooting ability had anything to do with his being picked to smoke out the missing man, Logan merely winked. We wish him well.

Henry returned the paper to Arthur, who was waiting greedily for his reaction. "Poor fellow," he said. "He's mad as a hatter. I did meet him, but I didn't realize he fancies himself rather comical. I reckon this is supposed to be a real knee slapper."

"Oh, no, Henry! You don't know Ben Ambrose," Allie exclaimed. "He's not being funny — he's playing a mean trick on you. In a town like this, every man under ninety thinks he's a sharpshooter, and a few claim to be gunmen. You'll be challenged, Henry. It's unfair. That terrible man!"

"Well, fine — I'll give 'em a show. Would you pass the turnips, Allie?"

"Are you as good as all that?" asked Arthur. "Did you really drill a lot of enemy soldiers?"

"Never killed a man in my life, Arthur. And I couldn't see a mosquito at a hundred yards, let alone hit its cigarette."

"My brothuh was with Beau-regard," said Miss Leisure. "And he told me he killed a whole pahrcel of Yankees. If y'all were a sharp-shooter," she added, "I don't see how y'all could avoid —"

"Easy: I missed them on purpose," Henry stated. "I'll swat flies and trap mice, but otherwise . . . Not that I don't love guns, ma'am — don't get me wrong. Actually, I had my own way of making war, which I won't go into now, but I don't have a lot of blood on my conscience."

But in Arthur B. Cleveland's knowing grin he saw doubt. "You musta said more than that to Ambrose," he suggested. "I don't reckon he'd flat out lie."

"Well — first time for everything," Henry said.

"Heard of General Miles Stockard, Henry?" Arthur asked. "I've seen him do tricks with a rifle that you wouldn't believe. He always insisted that every man in his outfit have a sharpshooter's medal."

"Why don't you tell him about me?" Henry said. "Set up a match. Anytime."

"Arthur," Allie said reprovingly. "Naughty."

Mr. Cleveland laughed. "Nope — no match. He lost the sight of his right eye in a shooting accident last year. Can't match-shoot at all now."

"What happened?"

"A shell blew up in the chamber, he said. Burned his face a little, blinded one eye. So we'll never know whether you coulda took him."

Henry winked at Allie. "Sit tight, Arthur — I'm going to show you something. Then you can kind of draw your own conclusion —"

He loosened his shoulders, shot his cuffs, sat straight up in the chair like a clairvoyant, and fished Allie's Mexican pesos from his pocket. He selected one without milling, with a good sharp edge, pulled the vinegar cruet to his place, and examined it. The cut-glass stopper had a perfectly flat top about the size of a nickel. Henry made sure the stopper was tight and level, then raised the cruet in his right hand and with care set the fat silver coin edgewise upon the stopper. The coin balanced there as though he had cast a spell on it.

"Merciful heaven!" whispered Miss Leisure. Henry rose and backed a couple of paces toward the window. The silver peso gleamed on the cruet. Allie chortled.

"Henry! Are you a stage magician?"

Henry said, "It's just a gift, like juggling. So it would be foolish to brag about it."

Then everyone started as a chiming crash like that of a bullet striking a church bell came from the porch. Miss Leisure's teacup clashed into her saucer, Arthur hissed a mild oath, and Allie, Henry was sure, gasped.

"*Jesus!*"

They all looked at Henry, who stood perfectly still with the peso still balanced on the vinegar cruet. He grinned, flipped the coin, and caught it.

"I reckon somebody hit your triangle a wallop with a gas pipe, Allie," he said. But then, through the vibrating echoes, he heard a small popping sound, familiar to anyone who knew guns.

Some prankster had hit the triangle with a .22 rifle slug.

As Allie moved to rise, he chuckled, then said, "Keep your seat, Allie. I imagine that's for me."

Wiping his lips, he went to the window and moved a curtain to peer out into the dusk. On the high ground across the road, silhouetted against a whiskey-colored sky, four men armed with rifles stood in a vacant lot. All appeared to be wearing the same style of black hat, and they were watching the house intently.

"Yes, ma'am — it's for me," he said. "I'll just pin notes to these boys' shirts and send them home to their wives."

"Aren't you going to take a gun?" Arthur asked.

"Why, I don't think I'll have to kill anybody, Arthur. We'll see." As he stepped onto the porch, one of the men on the low cliff bawled, "Bang! You're dead, gunman!" Then they all began yelling, "Bang! Bang! Bang!" "Make yer play, gunman!" "God's gift, hey?" and other nonsense.

Way out West, Henry thought, chuckling.

He walked into the rutted street and waited there while the men picked their way down the bank, laughing and hooting. One of them was Budge Gorman, the hound-faced man from the stable, still shirtless, his arms hairy as a tarantula's legs. The men lined up like rookies, guns pointed this way and that. The breeze brought Henry a light fragrance of spirits.

"Make your play, gunman!" the stableman said, pretending to make a hip-shot with his huge-bored rifle. All of the men wore black Grand Army hats with gold braid and the G. A. R. insignia on the front. Sears, Roebuck sold them for a dollar-ninety or so, Henry thought. Evidently they belonged to a shooting club.

"Took you long enough to get here, men," Henry said. "Still, the word in Kansas City is that Nogales men can't shoot for sour owl shit."

Budge Gorman bawled: *"That's a goddamn lie!"*

"As you were, Budge," Henry said firmly. "Detail — *attention!* Inspection — *arms!"*

Evidently all had been in the Army at some time, because they dressed their four-man line properly, went to port arms, and then to inspection arms.

One of the shooters, short, square-headed, and built like a stump, rattled open the bolt of his carbine. He was coatless and wore a tie and lavender sleeve garters.

"What's your name, soldier?" Henry asked.

"Leo Lucas — sir!"

"I want you all to watch as I perform the manual of arms, Black Jack Logan version dated 1885, per A. R. twenty-seven dash eighty-nine. I expect each and every one of you to be able to do it word-perfect tomorrow. . . ."

He smacked his palms up under the weapon to lift it off the stableman's hands, whirled the stock into the sky, and peered through the barrel, catching a circle of amber sunset. He tipped it this way and that to make the light run through the steel tunnel like a cleaning patch. The gun looked clean enough, but the barrel was slightly pitted. Henry worked the bolt rapidly, and the man grabbed at the fat brass shells as they flew.

Then, while they watched, he did his manual of arms, using the weapon as a drum major's baton, twirling and spinning it and finishing by throwing it high in the air and catching it. Then he smartly returned it.

"Detail — at *ease!*"

They burst into laughter, and Lucas pounded him on the back while introducing the others. "You know Budge Gorman — you left your horse at his stable. That's Elmo, the bean pole with the '95 Winchester and the beard, and the Model 90 takedown is Arnie. Henry, are you really the son of Captain Black Jack Logan of the Second Cavalry?"

"Yes, but I don't trade on his gifts. I'm my own man, Leo."

He gripped each man's hand, looking into his eyes as if for something important he had been seeking. Then he would smile briefly, pat his shoulder, and move on to the next.

"Well, gentlemen, it's a pleasure to meet some serious sharpshooters," he said. "But I'm flabbergasted that the marshal allows shooting in the streets.

"He don't! And we don't allow bragging, either!" Budge shouted.

"A disgusting habit," Henry agreed. "Who's

been bragging around here?"

"You!" the stableman shouted, poking a finger at him. "Ben Ambrose says you call yourself — you claim that you — How'd it go, Leo?" He squirmed with eagerness or a need to relieve himself.

"Yes, I was just reading it," Henry said "Your ed. and pub. seems to be a bit shell-shocked. What I told Ambrose was that I was a gun*smith* — not a gun*man.*"

"But you're looking for a killer, ain't you?"

"No. Simple telegrapher's mistake. But how Mrs. Parrish's telegram wound up in the hands of the newspaper editor, I don't know. That astonishes me."

"In this town," Leo Lucas said, "you have to come to grips with your astonishment. Word does get around. So you're a gunsmith, Henry. Don't you shoot at all?"

"Oh, indeed. I believe I'm a fair shot, and sometime when the light's better, let's tear up some targets."

Then he brought them to attention again and asked Budge: "What kind of gun you got there, trooper? I don't remember ever seeing anything quite like it. . . ."

Henry saw Elmo nudge Arnie, who was standing next to him, as Budge roared, "This here's a Remington Creedmoor, idiot! I paid fourteen seventy-five for it!"

"That's about right. What I meant, though, it's been altered."

He put his hands out and took the man's gun: Budge's face had reddened and he looked like a humiliated schoolboy as Henry inspected the Creedmoor.

"I'd be careful with that gun," Henry said, returning it.

"What's wrong with it?" Budge demanded, almost weeping.

"Well, what do you like to hunt? Baldwin locomotives on the wing? A .44 would have stopped anything you're ever going to meet. Now you're packing a gun that really isn't safe to fire."

"That's what I told him," the stumplike man said. "The metal's too thin, right?"

Better to have a friend than an enemy, Henry decided. He said, "I exaggerated a little, Budge. What I meant is that you'd better not use smokeless in this. Gunsmiths think twice before they modify a gun that's really about right to begin with. It's in my book, *The Law of the Gun,* which I'll give you all a copy of before I leave."

He inspected the other weapons, gave the shooters the compliments they were waiting for, but perceived that they were disappointed. They did not want the show to be over without a villain's having been dealt with.

And now that he was no longer the villain, they needed someone else to hiss at.

"Tell you what, boys," he said. "I'd like to shoot with you someday, but first I've got some business to tend to. I'll tell Budge when I'm free."

Leo Lucas scratched his neck. "Then I'd say you've got a problem, Henry. Because if you don't take care of this gunman business first, you won't get much other business done. Every time you go through a door, you're going to hear snickering. All I'm trying to say is, Ambrose has you in a box. We just shoot for fun, but other men are going to take it more serious. Like you'd insulted them. It's foolish, but you're going to have to do something, Henry. Show them you ain't a braggart — but you ain't afraid, either."

Henry sighed. "Yes, I suppose you're right. What if I were to challenge Ambrose to a shooting match? Would that —?"

"No, because Ben don't claim to be a marksman."

"Ah. Then maybe I should give him a lesson in journalism. If this was a joke, I think I ought to have a chuckle or two myself, don't you?"

The men perked up. "That's the ticket!"

"Wait here a minute," Henry said. "I'll tell

my landlady where I'm going, and I'll get my rifle."

"What kind you carry?" Budge shouted after him, unable to wait. Henry called, "Same as yours, Budge. The Model E, though — thirty-four-inch barrel, .44-105 bottleneck shells. Take the ash off a mosquito's cigarette at a hundred yards. . . ."

Chapter Eight

In the smoky dusk, Henry led the Grand Army of the Republic Shooting Club down the steep hill and turned south on International Street toward the stores, hotels, and saloons. Spread across the road in a skirmish line, the Grand Army was silent but charged up like a bottle of soda water, glancing often at him. Henry heard Budge Gorman give a happy chuckle and whisper to himself, "Goddamn."

A warm breeze from Mexico blew cool and steady in his face, and in this last half hour of daylight he could hear forage bells, church bells, and distant voices, and he savored the exciting atmosphere of the town, which gave him gooseflesh, like the first night in a foreign town, with different coins in his pocket, different odors in his nostrils, a different language. The woman he had met in the cemetery was a great part of this excitement, too.

Along the street, electric streetlights glowed

and pulsed in surges, as though somewhere a lame mule was generating electricity by stumbling around a pole. Nearing the newspaper office, the Grand Army fell silent. Did they fear they might distract the famous gunmaster at this crucial moment? he wondered.

Suddenly he noticed something that made him laugh. They looked at him.

"Men," he said, "I wonder if one of you soldiers can tell me why in hell we're walking down the middle of the street, like Wyatt Earp going to a shoot-out? Are sidewalks off-limits for shoot-outs?"

They voiced a little nervous laughter.

Then Henry said, "Leo?" and the man moved close to him. "Is this the kind of reporting Ambrose usually does?"

Leo held his rifle across his shoulder like a tramp's stick, front sight first. "Ben is as tricky as a blind bull, Henry. He persecuted Frances Parrish's father so cruelly — she was a Wingard, you see, Dr. Wingard's daughter — that he up and died."

Henry looked at him and wrinkled his nose in distaste. But be was loving it, finding out about Frances while discovering Ambrose's weak points.

"It was over the Narcotics Act. You know about it, of course."

"Put controls on narcotic substances? Yes, but what did Ambrose have to do with that?"

"Well, every last doctor in the country had his own pet syrup, or bitters, or whatnot, and every last concoction was laced with opium! Except Doc Wingard's. It had cocaine."

Budge Gorman put his face close to Henry's and bawled, "Henry, it was hell to pay when they took away all them drugs! Mrs. Ormsby's Bitters would cross your eyes and set you to singing 'Camptown Races.' And don't you know people was scurrying around like fire ants trying to find something just as good?"

Henry laughed. "No fooling!"

The tall, bearded man called Elmo said, "Dr. Wingard called his the Viennese Doctor's Wine of Coca. He was my doctor, and I used his concoction when I felt poorly. But he always said, 'Don't overdo it, Elmo — don't overdo any drug.' He was a fine man. Yes, indeed. But don't quote me. . . ."

Henry looked at him in disbelief. "Don't quote you? I think that's a pretty nice thing to say about a man."

"Uh, well — Ben's got everybody believing . . . I mean, nobody wants to stand out, do they?"

Henry put his rifle on his shoulder. "Okay, I've got it." And he thought with relish of how he was going to make the foppish publisher stand out that night.

As they walked, he was appraising each store they passed — a drugstore, several saloons, Proto Brothers' General Store, another drugstore called Chenoweth and Mix, a music store, a meat market. Complete little town, hidden away here on the border! Like a model, a creche.

"Why did he call it the . . . whatever?"

"Some recipe he read in a medical magazine. A famous Austrian doctor was boosting it as a tonic."

"A doctor for crazy people," Leo said. "A Dr. Freud, in Vienna. So Wingard compounded this coca stuff, no worse than anything else, and Ambrose took it — took quarts of it, Frances told me, after the trouble. Half the stuff he published made no goddamn sense at all. But when Doc Wingard wouldn't give him any more, he began printing stories about him selling it in secret! Wingard tried to sue him, but the court threw out the case. Oh, they was wild times in Nogales!"

"And then he died?" Henry prompted.

"Yes. He'd lost most of his patients. And a fine doctor, I reckon."

"But don't quote you?"

"Well . . . a lot of women cut Frances dead as well, and then after all that! — Ambrose

94

had the nerve to go to the doctor's graveside service!"

"No!" Henry looked at his rifle, as though to share with it the appalling story.

"And Frances slapped him in the face with his own bouquet! There was rose petals and cigar ash all over him. Ambrose has never forgiven her. Now it sounds like he's out to persecute *her.* "

"If that isn't that the damnedest, rottenest thing I ever heard. Come on, boys. I've got to hear Ambrose's side of the story. I hope for his sake he's got one."

He halted before the *Globe* office; it was on the left and the Frontera Hotel was on the right. Not far beyond, sprawled in a chair before the sentry box, a soldier sat puffing a pipe, a rifle leaning against the fence. Not much like guard duty in Cuba, thought Henry.

"Yonder's the newspaper office," said Leo Lucas. "Ben may not be there, but if he ain't, the general will be."

"That's Milo Stockard? Brave tracker of the wily Apache?" Henry was aware of being feverish. Was it malaria or excitement?

"Yes, sir," said Leo. "That's the old general. Tougher'n a night in a south Georgia jail."

Henry ran his eyes up and down the tall, narrow building, like a carpenter, maybe; or a demolitions expert deciding where to place his charges. Downstairs, a light burned behind the mullioned window. The name of the newspaper was emblazoned on the glass in gold leaf and boldly outlined in black. Above the walk, turning slightly in the breeze, the golden globe hung from a wooden boom extending over the sidewalk. In the final rays of the sunset it had the greenish look of a tarnished catalogue watch.

Rubbing the Winchester's gun stock thoughtfully, Henry said, "Why don't you boys have a beer while I talk to Ambrose? I don't want him to say he was outmanned."

They scattered, one of the Grand Army men hurrying into the hotel and the others heading for saloons, obviously planning to pass the word that the famous Kansas City gunman was calling Ambrose's bluff. He swung the loading lever down and back to punch the first of fifteen shells into the chamber with a slick, oily sound; a fat .44-105 bottleneck shell was now hammer-ready, a cartridge nearly as large as his index finger. He snapped his fingers and set his feet apart.

"Ben Ambrose!" he shouted. "You lying gasbag! Get your polecat carcass out here!" Is that wild Western enough? he wondered.

A man came into the doorway and stared at him, his sleeves rolled up and a printer's stick in his hands. He was a short, bandy-legged, grizzled old badger of a man with a bald head and a black patch over one eye, and he was Captain Logan's old commanding officer.

He's not here, friend!" he called. "But do you know who I am?"

"Yes, sir. Indeed I do. Do you know me?"

"Reckon I do! You're Black Jack Logan's boy!"

"No, sir, I'm just plain Henry Logan. It's between Ambrose and me. My father don't come into it."

"Suit yourself. Come back tomorrow morning."

"I will. But I beg to leave a message."

"Shoot," the general said.

"Right, General! Right in the old ten-ring. That's exactly what I had in mind."

He squeezed the gun stock between his biceps and ribs and fired the first crashing shot without aiming. The general yelled and ducked. After the golden lightning flash of flame, the thunderclap that followed shook windows all along the street. He heard horses snorting and stamping.

The golden globe resounded with a loud *whanggg!* It leapt and began to swing, while glittering strips and sequins of gold leaf drifted in the air. On the hotel veranda, men were laughing and yelling and stamping on the wooden deck.

Henry bared his teeth, snapped another shell into the chamber, and started a deafening rapid-fire fusillade.

The big metal ball rocked and swung; it clanged and thumped against the front of the shop as the big blunt-nosed slugs hammered at it, caving it in, tearing pieces of tin loose. Ambrose's personal world lurched and danced, banged hollowly, and shed gilt in patches like sunburned skin, or butterflies, or certain kinds of fireworks.

The smoke from the gunfire generated some coughing, and Henry's ears rang. He was aware that the hotel veranda was clustered with yelling, howling, laughing men, while others lined the walks bawling encouragement. With only a few shells left, he lowered the gun and flexed his shoulders. Inside the newspaper office he could see the general standing coolheaded, arms crossed, waiting.

Looking almost pensive, Henry rocked another shell into the chamber, his eyes on the swinging wreckage of the sphere, his front sight trailing it back and forth like a metronome, but with the gun still at the offhand position. At the precise moment, he squeezed off the shot. The globe was ripped from the boom to which it was bolted.

A man bawled, *"There she goes!"*

The globe made an arching flight and landed in the street. It bumped along a few yards and came to rest in the dirt. Henry pulled the loading lever down and threw the breech open, like an antagonist offering another man his hand after some bitter words.

"General?" he called.

Stockard came to the walk, still clutching the printer's stick, and he looked unruffled.

"The hell you aren't Black Jack's boy!" he shouted. "Now, if I ever knew a Logan, you'll get drunk on Bushmill's and sing till sunup!"

"I said I was my own man. I'm going home and clean my rifle. Tomorrow we can talk about the kind of man Ambrose is."

Chapter Nine

His ears still ringing, Henry poured water from a pitcher into a basin, scrubbed the powder-smoke grime from his hands, and then used the soapy water to sluice out the barrel of his gun. Afterward he ran oily patches through it and wiped the gun with affection. He chuckled as he put it away in its case.

Then he noticed a small religious postcard lying on the white candlewick bedspread.

He picked it up. It represented a crucifix, more gruesome than most he had seen, with great gouts of blood running down Christ's body and face and a crown of thorns like barbed wire. Was Allie the religious person who was slipping the message to him? More likely Miss Leisure was the culprit; who, however, was bound to be a Southern Baptist. So who was his secret pal? He turned the card. A message was written in careful handwriting on the reverse, but the language of the author was Spanish.

Yawning, Henry trudged down the hall to the kitchen, where he found Alice Gary washing up the supper things with the help of the same little Mexican girl who had led him to his room. "Hey, Allie!" he said, and she started and looked at him.

"Henry! Thank heaven! I heard a lot of shooting. . . ."

"We had a little turkey shoot down there," Henry said. "I was wondering if you could translate this for me."

Allie looked at both sides of the card and spoke to the girl. The girl whispered in her ear, twisting at a chocolate-brown braid and rubbing her knees together.

"She says a boy brought it from Father Vargas, at the Catholic church. That's on the other side, the other Nogales. It says, let's see . . . 'Esteemed — dear — Señor Logan, please to, to . . . please do me the favor of, of to visit me . . . at the church, as fast, as *early* as you can. *Mañana!*' — know that one? You'll learn it! — 'on negotiations . . . no, business, of the more great, greatest delicacy. . . .' Well! have you been sparking some Mexican lady?"

"No, ma'am! I don't get this," Henry said. "Is my soul a matter of the greatest delicacy?" He scrached his armpit, yawned again.

Allie said she didn't savvy, either. Henry said, "I reckon it'll keep till *mañana,*" and went to bed.

Roosters, donkeys, dogs, and bells, wagon tires grinding along the street, horses clopping, and finally a train whistle down the hill woke Henry early the next morning. The window curtain glowed with the clear rose of an Arizona dawn. He groped for his watch, squinted, and saw that it was five-forty. Still groggy, he sat up, wound the Ingersoll, and began to feel sudden excitement about the day ahead.

By the time he had shaved, breakfast was ready. Arthur Cleveland was eager to hear about the shoot-out, but Henry offered no news. Finally Arthur said, "I hear you shot the windows out of the newspaper office! Drove Stockard clean out the back door!"

Henry hooted. "Come on, Arthur — you must have read that in the *Globe.* I just gave a shooting demonstration. Pass the butter, please."

In the warm morning he sauntered down the hill. Smoke from breakfast fires brimmed in the basin. People were going to work on horses, in buggies, and on foot. He decided to walk and headed south on International

Street, underneath the wooden awnings. Passing the *Globe* office, he could see two men inside. The remains of the globe had been carried away, and most of the gold leaf was gone.

At the ten-strand barbed-wire fence, a yawning sentry on the American side waved him on. There was no guard on the Mexcan side, and he wandered into the village, noting similarities to pueblos in Cuba. The stony hills rising on either side looked skinned, rockier than those of the Fort Bowie areas, and the town itself resembled a camp, the street irregularly defined by pitted dirt walks. What awnings he saw were made of cactus wands supported by crooked poles, and all the buildings were constructed of unplastered adobe bricks. Dogs and children were setting up a racket everywhere, while burros trotted north with loads of firewood. Women in black dresses, with black rebozos over their heads, hurried along with buckets of water drawn up from a pump somewhere.

He saw no church steeple, but finally, peering down an alley, spotted a high whitewashed wall, perfectly plain, but with a round belfry rising from behind it and a deep blue sky setting off the tower.

He walked through the alley to the wall and passed through an opening in the church wall to a bleak forecourt outlined by small white-washed rocks, a few cactus growing in this defined area. The building itself looked as solid as the Alamo. The walls were thick; the big, iron studded double door was set several feet back to firm a sort of alcove. As he was looking for a bell to ring, a priest in a black cassock parted the tall doors and greeted him by name.

"Señor Logan? Thank you for coming, sir. I am Father Vargas. Please come in. "

The priest's hand felt cold and fragile in Henry's. Vargas was a small man of about forty who had a look of nervous intensity, the pallor and half frown of a man who often had stomach trouble. As he stepped back into the church, one thin hand massaged the other, as though comforting it. He was, Henry believed, a very troubled man.

"If you will follow me . . ."

Henry trailed him into the fragrant dusk of the church. "You speak English but you don't write it?"

"Not a word! But I trusted you would get the letter translated somehow."

Inside, the church was lighted by a few candles in sconces; near the altar at the rear, a tableful of votive candles provided haven. The air was cold and dusty, heavy with incense.

Father Vargas opened a door and Henry walked into a small office furnished with little more then a desk and chair; a second chair, tall and crude-looking, appeared much too upright to be comfortable. An ivory crucifix hung against the adobe wall, a silver candelabrum holding three candles lighting it. Vargas indicated the uncomfortable chair. Henry sat down, thinking, actually, about Frances Parrish. Had she been married here? If she were on the outs with the churches of Nogales as well as the people, she might have been. Vargas's fingers patted the desktop and his mournful eyes finally came to Henry's.

"Señor," he said, "I am in a ghastly dilemma! I face the most barbarous decision of my life!"

Henry grinned. "So naturally you sent for a gunsmith."

"You might be surprised at how much you can help, Mr. Logan. I could write my bishop, but it would take a month for the letter to reach him, and then another month for his answer to come. And there is simply not that much time!"

Henry tried to get comfortable on the chair, which was short in the seat and had a tilt that kept him crouching forward as though he were about to rise.

"Would it be a good guess that you read

about me somewhere?" he asked.

Vargas patted a newspaper on the desk. "I immediately wrote the note to you."

"I'm sorry, Father Vargas, but it's hogwash! Throw the paper away. Wrap meat in it. I came to Arizona as a favor to a lawyer friend. I simply need to find this man, Parrish, and get an explanation of why he doesn't answer his letters."

The priest was shaking his head. "You won't find him, Señor Logan. And that is no hogwash."

Touched by an uneasy hunch, Henry said, "Why not?"

"Because, sir, Señor Reep is dead!"

Henry's spirits soared into the air like a hawk. "Are you positive?"

"A woman in my parish told me she saw him shot to death. *Una puta, you see.*"

Henry knew the word from Cuba; it meant "prostitute." "A pity. I suppose an, er, whorehouse fight?"

"Not exactly . . ."

Henry waited, pleased yet puzzled. His own problem was solved, and in the best possible manner. But he did not see why a whorehouse murder should cause the priest such distress, nor why he had sent for him.

"Is that your cruel dilemma?" he asked.

"No señor. Not precisely. Señor Reep was

a jolly man, and he gave me the candelabrum you see behind me, although he is not a Catholic. *Was* not. I admire his wife very much — excuse me, his widow. I wish Frances would come to see me. Perhaps I could help the poor lady."

"Oh? Does Frances have a problem, too?" (Of course! She was a widow. Henry just happened to view this tragedy differently.)

"Ah, señor! A most grave problem, indeed. According to the woman who told me this, Frances is the one who shot him!"

"Oh, my God!" Henry said.

Numbed, he sat staring at the priest. He started to say some thing, but his throat was dry and he made a croaking sound. "Excuse me. No, Father, this woman must be as crazy as Ben Ambrose! What would Frances be doing in — in such a place?"

"I didn't say she was, Señor Logan. The woman said that she lived with Señor Reep for several weeks last year, at the place on his ranch that they call Spanish Church. He was digging for treasure, she said."

Henry squinted at the silver candlestick on the wall. For some reason he felt very skeptical of the ornament, and he wanted to see this bit of treasure dug up by a man now dead. He crossed the floor to the little flickering shrine and examined the candle stick. The handwork was hold, the decoration crude, the silver pitted. A date was engraved on the underside of it: 1723. The artifact looked disappointingly genuine.

"Is this something Rip is supposed to have dug up?"

"I don't know, sir. He gave it to me . . . oh, I suppose a year ago."

"Just how did the woman's fairy tale go?"

"Well, according to her, Frances rode out to Spanish Church last August and caught them together. Cata — this woman, I should say — rode her burro away. But she got trapped in a box canyon and had to ride back an hour later. Rip was sitting beside his campfire, in the dark now, playing his banjo, when the woman heard a shot and saw him fall to the ground. She rode off into the dark. She was sure she wasn't seen."

His mind squirming like a jail-house lawyer, Henry detected a sour note here, and he raised his finger. "Wait. It's dark, right? She hears a shot — and she says Frances fired the gun. Why? Did she actually *see* her shoot?"

"She says she saw it all. I'm inclined to believe her. She was as distressed by the murder as I was. We all love Frances — Panchita, as we call her. She speaks better Spanish than most Mexicans, in fact, and has nothing but friends here. Her father took care of many of us. Panchita has often nursed our own sick people."

"What kind of gun was it?"

"A revolver, she told me. She'd seen it hanging in the little rock house out there. It belonged to Reep. A very beautiful weapon — if that is not a contradiction."

Thinking sharp and hard, Henry replaced the candlestick. "Has she told anyone else?"

"No. She told me in the confessional."

Aha! "Then how can you tell me this, Father? Or anyone else? Isn't there a . . . you know, a canonical law . . .?"

"Of course. But the woman came to me again just a few days ago. Now she wants me to write a letter to the sheriff for her to sign, telling about the murder! She's afraid of being arrested for adultery if she goes over there."

"Did she say what happened to the body?"

The priest looked surprised. "No — no, she didn't, come to think of it. And I didn't think to ask." He shrugged. "Apparently it was dragged away, or buried."

"By Frances? Come on, Father, you know as well as I do that she's not a cold-blooded —"

"No, I'm sure she isn't. You have a point. . . . I'll ask the woman about that."

"I think I would, Father! I mean, *no body?*

Ha! Then how could a murder charge be brought?"

Henry followed his lead on down the dim trail.

This crazy fellow, this Rip Parrish, gambler and roustabout, had been living with a Mexican woman while Frances had tried to run the ranch alone. Frances had caught him redhanded. Then — maybe — she'd had to defend herself against him. Maybe he'd been drunk — had tried to beat her. And possibly the quarrel had wound up with her accidentally shooting him.

Maybe.

The priest was speaking softly.

"What?" Henry asked.

"La problema," said the padre, "is that murder usually comes to light. But I respect this woman so much that I can't report it! Yet I must! Do you see?"

"Yes, I see. But I don't understand about the body!"

"I don't, either. But there's an old mine there. Someone could have dragged it inside and covered it with rocks. Otherwise the buzzards —"

"In Spanish, do you have our saying, 'Let sleeping dogs lie'?"

"I'm afraid this dog will wake up, sooner or later. The woman will tell one of her lovers from the other side, and the lover will tell Sheriff Bannock. And the sheriff is not a friend of Panchita's. Her father did a little operation on his throat once, and now — now his bellows can't be heard across the room — he can only whisper. He blames the doctor. But he always had a husky voice, and he barbecues his throat with cigars — twenty a day, they say!"

Henry was looking at the candlestick again. "Wouldn't you think," he said, "that handing old church ornaments around would give people the idea that there's treasure there?"

"I suppose. I've made no secret of it."

"So that he'd be taking the risk of having his treasure stolen, or being murdered, wouldn't he? Doesn't that seem peculiar?"

"Yes, it does!"

Smiling, Henry rested his palms on the desk and leaned toward the priest. "Want to know what I'd do?" he asked.

"Tell me!"

Henry straightened. "Nothing!" Then he raised both arms melodramatically. "Nothing at all! I wouldn't lift a finger, Father. I'd hold my peace. Why not talk to Frances? Maybe the Mexican woman hates her. Maybe Frances really read her the articles of war out there. Would it be surprising? Damn woman stealing her husband?

"So this woman may come back one of these

days to confess again — that she lied! — you see? And, my *God,* Padre, if you've told the sheriff, then Frances is in jail and maybe she'll never be the same. Didn't they hang a woman in the Yuma prison a while back? I read about it. So whatever you do, don't tell Whispering George. I'll talk to Frances," he announced. "And I'll let you know what I find out."

"Bless you! It's exactly what I hoped for. Here — please take this rosary to Panchita for me, and ask her to visit me someday soon."

Henry looked it over, a rather lumpy silver necklace, and dropped it in his pocket with a wry smile. "Well, I was baptized a Presbyterian or something, but what the hell. Be glad to."

And just what am I going to say to Frances? Henry thought, plodding back through the dark church. Interesting how people who had a cruel burden to bear usually managed to hang it on somebody else. In fact, the situation was almost humorous. *I'm going to ride out there to Spanish Church with her, and she's going to tell me the true story according to her — which according to this Mexican woman was a pack of lies!*

He looked at his watch. Time to have it out with Ben Ambrose and the fine old Apache-murdering general. . . .

PART TWO

THE
HUNTER

Chapter Ten

An hour before his rendezvous with Frances Parrish, Henry rapped on the door of the *Globe*. Glum with misgivings, he had plodded north from the Catholic church among burros overloaded with desert firewood. Children switching them along pointed at the red-haired man in the undertaker's suit and laughed. Making quick draws, he cocked and fired his thumb at them; without, however, feeling very playful.

He sensed that he was being watched from inside the newspaper office; and perhaps from the hotel, whose guests he had given such an exciting evening. He turned his head: Men seated along the shaded hotel porch were indeed aware of him. He gazed up and down the street. A wagon was unloading beer barrels before Brickwood's Saloon; businessmen, cattlemen, and professional men were on the walks, many heading for the hotel. From the railroad yard came a series of short, sharp hoots. As he was about to rap again, a lock rasped, a man coughed, the door was yanked open, and General Stockard was staring at him.

Stockard, grinning, gestured with his cigar. "Come in, Logan, come in!"

Henry went as far as the doorsill, checking the interior of the shop for the general's foppish and possibly dangerously emotional partner. In the glare of a hissing carbide ceiling fixture, he saw a printing press with iron scrollwork like that of a sewing machine, a walnut box telephone resting on the desk, a stick of type lying on a marble slab, and long galley proofs hanging from hooks in the wall. But there was no sign of the editor.

Stockard gave a harsh laugh. "Relax, Henry! Ben'll be along. He's not dangerous. Probably having a cup of coffee across the street. Care to step over and have a cup? Or a whiskey? Like to show off my famous gunman-guest."

Henry shook his head. Entering the cool building after the hot street was like slipping back into early spring. The dry, chilly air felt good on his skin. The general looked him over, chuckling.

"Brave man, though, Henry! Walking unarmed into a place you shot up last night!"

Henry smiled, extended his right arm, and

116

looked at it, with the impression of a magician proving there was nothing up his sleeve. "What gave you the idea I was unarmed?" He gave his arm a hitch, the right cuff slipped back, and for an instant the silver, over-and-under barrels of a derringer gleamed. Then he performed the same magic with his left sleeve.

"Ha! That's the stuff!" Stockard cried. He planted himself beside a desk, his chin up and his one green eye sharp as acid. He was a tough and grizzled old warrior, and with the patch over his right eye he looked like a desperado. His head was bald, his jaws frizzed with badgerlike gray hairs as were his ears, and his eye looked as though it should be in the eye socket of some predatory animal. His skin was thin and shiny, blemished with liver spots.

Suddenly he smashed his hands together. "By God, Henry — if we haven't got a parcel of things to talk about! Let me look at you! Black Jack Logan's own son! Your father would have been proud of you."

Henry dropped into the office chair at one of the desks. "For a little show like that? No, sir. For what your partner did, my father would have burned this place down, with Ben hanging from the pole. Somebody's going to give that popinjay an Apache haircut one of these days, General. Yet the town seems afraid of him! What's the secret?"

"Come on, Henry — you mustn't take Ben too seriously. Nobody does. Ben fancies himself a Horace Greeley. Making newspaper history out here where half the subscribers can't read — they just want to impress the neighbors by having the paper on the front porch. Well, how is your mother, Henry? Remarried, I suppose?"

"Yes — to a gunsmith. I was eighteen when he died and took over the shop. Mother died three years ago."

"Ah, pity. My own wife — did you know Emily? You were pretty young."

"I used to see her at the post."

"Well, when you do meet her, she'll ask you four times a minute what church you go to!" And the general laughed. "Sad, though. When we lost our home to that double-dealing cardsharp, Humboldt Parrish, she began to fail. But, hell, that's water under the bridge."

Suddenly the general leaned forward and peered into Henry's fice, leaned back and laughed. "Judging by your complexion," he said, "you saw a bit of the Cuban campaign. What was your outfit?"

"Teddy's own. Armorer."

"Found yourself a nice, safe spot, didn't you? Hiding in a tent! Damn these armchair cavalrymen!" Still grinning, chomping on the crooked cigar, trying to get Henry's goat now, he waited for his response.

Henry said, "I also climbed trees and let them shoot at me."

"That's more like it. Too bad you didn't shoot that mosquito that drilled you, since you say you can take the ash off one's cigarette. The latest theory is that malaria is caused by the sting of certain mosquitoes."

"Is that a fact?"

Stockard leaned over to spit into a cuspidor. "Personally," he said, "I think it's rubbish. I've been bit by every kind of insect in the Western Hemisphere, and never had a fever. In fact, I've never been sick a day in my life. Don't touch medicine, either, though I take certain Indian remedies that keep my bowels regular and my kidneys flushed out."

"There's no medicine for accidents, though, is there?" Henry said. "I suppose some woman clawed your eye out, since it certainly wasn't man nor beast." He wanted to find out whether the general's explanation of his eye patch tallied with that of the Grand Army men.

Stockard lazily waved at a rack of guns above a desk, a mere series of pegs set into the adobe wall. Above them hung a yellow-and-black pennant, apparently the general's old headquarters guidon. "My own damned fault," he said with a sigh. "I was changing the load in a smokeless shell so's I could use the Remington up there without blowing my head off. I like a .50-caliber express shell for lions-870 grains of lead."

Henry raised his brows, got up and took the rifle from the pegs on the plastered wall. He puffed the dust from it and looked it over. The rifle was a Remington #3 Long Range, .40-110 caliber. A .40 wasn't .50 even in Arizona, and besides — amused, he looked at Stockard.

"This is .40-caliber," he said.

Stockard shrugged. "Forty, .50, what's the difference? Since I had to give up shooting —" He spat in the cuspidor.

"But why in thunder do you need such a fistful of lead for lions?"

Bridling, Stockard curled his upper lip back from his teeth. "Lion or Apache, trooper, the order is to take your game down. What do you use for lions?"

"A saucer of milk," Henry said. "Hell, mountain lions won't bother you! Just stand your ground and say, 'Here, kitty, kitty!'" And he colored his laugh with a slightly jeering note.

He heard Stockard muttering, and, content that he had stung him, replaced the rifle on the pegs and lifted down a second, a '92 Winchester .22. Under the dust it was an unremarkable piece; he was surprised that the general would own a small-caliber plinking gun. He balanced it on its pegs again and put his palm under the third. And knew in a flash that it was Stockard's favorite gun.

An 1885 Winchester, it was a .45 target rifle, and its condition was the first indication of its status — like the favored horse in a livery stable that always shone with grooming. No dust dulled the blued steel, discolored from the heat of long target sessions, nor the rich, oiled walnut of the stock. The piece was heavy, its thirty-inch octagonal barrel the heaviest Winchester made. The sidewalls were high and thick. When he worked the loading lever, the falling block dropped with an oily whisper to expose the chamber. The barrel had been tapped for a telescope sight, and he saw the leather case of a full length scope resting on wall pegs.

"Very nice gun," he said. "Army-issue?"

"Single-shot? No, no."

The question had been automatic, because his fingertip had just encountered a rough slot in the metal, where the flaming pot of ordnance would be. "Of course." Henry squinted and saw the letters *BB* and a tiny date. He knew what it meant but did not comment.

However, his little finger slipped into the chamber, like an officer's on inspection, and he found where the Browning brothers, of Ogden, Utah, had transformed the .45-caliber to .50. But a little farther down, it narrowed to .45 again. It now took bottlenose ammunition. He had no idea why the change had been made, but it was the target rifle of a man who took his shooting seriously.

"A man told me you were reloading black-powder shells to smokeless when you — lost your eye," he said. "Maybe it was just as well you didn't finish. This gun won't handle smokeless powder very long. Might've blown your head off."

"Don't believe all they tell you in armorer's school."

Henry worked the loading lever again. "Which is your lion gun?"

"The Remington."

Henry looked at him. "You don't mean to say you push 870 grains of lead in that?"

"No! That's another gun — it's at home." Stockard barked a laugh. "Never argue with an armorer! Mouth like a damned encyclopedia. Since the accident I can't shoot, anyway. So what the hell."

Then the general rather ceremoniously set fire to a fresh cigar, with the born commander's implied air of demanding attention, finally sitting on the edge of the desk and focusing his eye on Henry until he was satisfied he had his man. He said solemnly: "There is something I have to tell you, Henry. It never went into the reports after your father's death, and only a few other men and I know about it. I didn't believe your mother should know, and I'm grateful to have the chance to tell you now."

Henry replaced the Winchester and waited.

"When I stood in the ashes of that barn, trying to distinguish one of my cremated troopers from another, I said to my first sergeant, 'We will take five Apache lives for each life the Apache took here. I will not retire until the job is done.' And, Henry — I succeeded! Your father's life was paid for to the last Apache hide! Forty heathen Indians! One here, a couple of others there . . ."

Stricken, Henry stared into the parched old face. "You're not serious."

"You bet I am!" He clapped Henry's shoulder.

Henry stood up. "How in God's name did you know who committed the massacre? That was Yaqui country as well as Apache. Not to mention outlaws! The treasure was never found, and Indians didn't give a damn for money. My God, General, do you understand what you've done?"

Stockard opened his mouth to speak, closed it, and suddenly snatched the cigar from his mouth. He looked at it and hurled it at Henry. It struck his chest, leaving ash on his clean white shirt.

"Understand?" he roared. "I understand, but you don't! You haven't seen the dead and tortured men and women! You haven't risked your life to put those savages in the corrals where they belonged. Ranchers are safe here now, and the Indian respects us. Not because of mollycoddles like you, but because men like me and Crook and Miles put our lives on the line!"

The little bell over the door tinkled and Ben Ambrose entered.

The editor halted in the doorway and glowered at Henry. He made his twisted cigar fume, his lips emitting little puffs of smoke. His face was as brown and dry as jerked beef, and Henry thought of a mummy he had seen in a museum.

"You miserable son of a pariah dog!" Ambrose said.

Henry studied him like some curious creature he did not recognize: a wheeled lizard, a flying dog. And he shook his head in wonder.

"Listen to yourself, man! That's terrible talk. Isn't this the country where a man can get shot for opening his mouth? I thought I let you down very easy."

Ambrose threw his cigar at the cuspidor, dropped behind his desk, and glared on in a bitter silence.

Henry sighed. "Ambrose," he said, "I've been trying to understand something, and I think maybe I've got it. You've had things your way so long, people think you're dangerous. You make noises like a bull canary, and people think they'd better give you room. Then a man like me comes along and you insult him, and he doesn't know he's supposed to grin and do a barnyard shuffle. You see? Well, I'm sorry about ruining that big gold apple of yours, but I had to let people know I'm not the braggart you said I was. You put me in a tough spot. Don't you see?"

Ambrose tensed, leaning forward. "I see that you've put *me* in one now . . . it's not over. It's just started."

The general said roughly, "Forget it, Ben. You blundered, and you paid for it. Let's get down to business. Get the maps."

From a rack Ambrose brought a sheaf of maps hanging like drying bed sheets. His face sullen, he brushed away some paste pots and litter on a composing table and flopped the maps down, then went to stand and stare out the window into the street.

General Stockard rustled impatiently through the maps, found the one he wanted, and banged down slugs of type to anchor the corners. "Stand here, where you can see. Now, pay attention. . . ."

The map bore the proud emblem of the U.S. Army Topographic Command and covered the area of the Mexican border from the Huachuca Mountains twenty miles east of Nogales to the Pajarito Mountains about the same distance west. Southward, the world appeared to end at Nogales, for below the border all was white paper. Curious to see where he had been, where he was, and where he was going, Henry leaned over the map. Stockard jabbed a finger at a grid intersection.

"Hackberry Spring — then straight up the river. Two hours' ride. My land — whoops, Parrish's land! — starts there, right at the river, some of the old Baca Land Grant. Runs west through twenty miles of hellish canyons, mesquite jungles, mesas, and rattlesnake dens, and rims out at the Tres Amigos Mountains. Water, water everywhere — except at the ranch house, where you have to carry it by bucket from a *pozo* up on the mesa. I was doing beautifully, Logan . . ."

The general's finger roved the map, here and there and back again, sausagelike, rigid as a stick, the finger of an old farmer.

"I got the Engineers to do me an irrigation plan and build me a bunkhouse like a barracks — and the house! Oh, you'll see it, the woman will take you through it, proud as a peahen! My wife planted the things she loves, peonies, roses, wisteria — I told you her mind's going — never been the same since she had to pack and leave so that foul gambler could move in! My dream — I've had to scale it down a bit — is to have Emily die in her own home. In the four poster bed I brought from Vermont."

Henry said, "Were you thinking of her when you bet your ranch in a crap game?"

Ambrose turned to shout, "His partner lost it for him! The damned fool was going to Denver to buy cattle! Why don't you shut up and listen?"

Henry smiled. "That's different. You just gave him the deed — and let him hop a rattler, with the ranch in his pocket."

"He had power of attorney to borrow on it," Stockard said. "As much as he needed to buy the cattle. He's never been seen in the Territory since. But that's neither here nor there. I've decided to buy the ranch back. I'll pay you to act as my agent."

He took an envelope and tossed it before Henry. Smiled and bobbed his head. Henry left it there. Stockard pushed it toward him.

"I'm not trying to hoodwink her," he said. "But I can't persuade her — she won't listen to me. Just give her that envelope. Make damned sure she reads what's in it. It lays everything out so that even a female can understand it.

"There's a hundred for you if she accepts," he added.

"Why should she listen to me?"

Stockard leaned forward, confidentially. "The woman's alone, Henry! It's not natural for a woman not to have a man around to keep her mind straight. Mrs. Parrish desperately needs somebody to tell her what to do. And she feels it! Give her a couple of days and she'll be asking you which skirt she should wear, how to fix the pump, and whether to sell the ranch."

Ambrose snorted. "And then she'll wear a different skirt and tell you the pump's all right now. And she's decided to keep the ranch."

"She won't keep it long," said the general. "She owes everybody in the county. As soon as Rip's declared legally dead, they can sue and not look bad. What do you say?"

"Nothing. I happen to think her husband may still be alive. When I find him, or his body, I'm through here."

Ambrose showed his long yellow teeth.

"That should be a snap, Logan. Just sift the sands of Sonora until you find where the *bandidos* left the carcass."

"Something like that. Everybody knows he's dead. Well, everybody but our whispering buffoon of a sheriff." He stormed toward some smudged galley proofs hanging from hooks on the wall. "Read this! I'm running the story tomorrow."

He yanked loose a long galley proof and shoved it at Henry. "This is how the town feels! The whole Rip Parrish picture is right there."

Henry laid the galleys atop the map.

RECALL MOVE GROWS!
Angry Nogalenos held a meeting Tuesday night to consider legal steps to remove Sheriff George "Whispering George" Bannock from office.

Sheriff Bannock, recently reelected to a third term, was invited to attend the meeting but failed to appear. Citizens of Santa Cruz County had hoped to hear his explanation of why he has not taken steps to declare Richard I. Parrish legally dead.

Henry dropped the galleys. "He could be in Mexico City," he said. "San Francisco,

Denver, El Paso. Wherever there's a poker game going on. Declaring him dead isn't exactly like making a weather prediction."

Stockard bobbed his bald head. "Maybe you're right. Maybe it's best that you go out there and look things over — see the mess he left her. If you agree with me that a woman can't handle a ranch where border hoppers, treasure hunters, and Mexican cow thieves come and go like it was a hotel, then for God's sake persuade her to sell!"

Chapter Eleven

In the wide entrance to Budge Gorman's stable, his dog lay Sphinx-fashion in the shade, snapping at flies; but Budge was not in sight. A horseshoe hung from a hitch rail, a railroad spike dangling from the horseshoe. Henry rang it and it produced a thin chiming in a class with Budge's hee-heeing laugh. In the barn Budge called, "Yo!" and in a moment he emerged leading Henry's horse and carrying his saddle and pad on his shoulder. After looping the lead rope around the rack, he dropped the saddle on the horse's back, set his black hat on his brow, and stared at Henry with a wild expression.

"Hear you're leaving us!" he said.

"For a while, Budge."

"Don't make any damn sense, Logan! Haul in town one day, leave the next. What's the matter with you?"

Henry tapped the horseshoe again. Listening to it hum, he said thoughtfully, "Funny, isn't it? Maybe I'm restless. I don't know."

"Well, I don't know, either. I expect you don't like Nogales. Most city people don't. Think they're too damn good for us."

"Hey!" Henry protested, gripping Budge's shoulder. "I think this place is just right. I like a town you can shoot up and get away with it."

Budge began his hissing laugh. "What did Ambrose do?"

"Oh, he told me not to do it again. What's the bad news?"

"Two-fifty. Gave him some molasses 'n' oats."

No wonder the horse was pawing the dirt, Henry thought — inaction and rich food after three days riding the rods. "Did you check his hoofs?"

Budge dug in his overalls pocket for a hoof pick. "Keep your shirt on. Might I ask where you're off to?"

"Yonder — up the river a piece."

"Better let me draw you a map, then. Man can get lost up yonder. Feller I know ain't been seen for months." Budge's windy laugh said he knew exactly what Henry was up to.

Henry grinned. "I'm just going out to look at ranch land. I have a friend in K. C. who's interested in acquiring a ranch hereabouts.

Thought Spider Ranch might suit him."

"It's mighty good land," Budge said. "Fine stands of grama and poverty grass. But that ranch is too far out for a single lady."

"Are we talking about the same lady? I thought she was married."

Budge chuckled. "Not so's you could notice it! Not lately. Rip's dead and buried, if I know gamblin' men."

"Frances will be meeting me here directly," Henry said.

"I know that! She's picking up some freight at the depot." Budge glared at him and dropped the hoof pick in his pocket. Then he peered up the street and muttered: "Need some advice, Henry."

"Gun problem?"

Budge took a breath. "Business problem."

"Man, you have no idea how little I know about business! I'm just an ignorant gunsmith. If it can't be improved with gun oil, a screwdriver, and a rag, forget it."

"Well, all's I really need is a feller to write something down for me."

"Fine, then. I write a pretty good hand."

Budge went into the barn and emerged in seconds with a ruled letter pad and a pencil. He placed them on the horse's back.

"I've got a mechanical pencil," Henry said, reaching in his coat. The stableman grabbed a brush and began grooming the horse, as Henry meticulously adjusted the pencil.

"There's some prices first," said Budge. "I promised to buy Frances some feed — it's wicked how they rob her. Here's the figures. . . ."

Henry knelt cowboy-fashion, writing tablet on his knee. "Fire at will. This thing does numbers, too."

Budge recited some figures on feed and salt blocks. "Got that?"

"Now, this goes on another page." Budge moved quickly to the off side of the horse, where Henry could not see him. As he brushed, in a cloud of dust and dander, he began muttering, so low that Henry had to strain to hear him.

"Little louder," he called.

"'Dear Frances,'" Budge dictated. "'You must know I like you. It don't matter a bit to me the lies they tell about you —'"

Anguished, Henry said, "Hold on, cowboy! Wouldn't it be better if you — ah — told her this, instead of my writing it down? You don't want to be like Captain John Smith, do you?"

"The Army has nothing to do with this, idiot! I've been figuring for weeks, but I can't ask none of my friends to write it down."

"All right." Henry sighed. "Suit yourself I'll keep it to myself, too."

"Okay, here we go. 'I know you're an honest woman, Frances, and I liked your father. I want you to know . . .' No, back up. Say this: 'I wish to talk to you when I bring the grain out. Respectfully . . .'"

By the time Henry had finished writing, Budge was ready with a small, smudged envelope on which an earlier address had been crossed out. "Give this to her sometime today."

"Here she comes," Henry said.

Budge slipped into the barn.

Chapter Twelve

Henry climbed up into the buggy and tried to take the reins, but Frances shook her head. "Not here, thank you. Heavens! In *this* town? After we're on the road you can spell me."

"I'll ride shotgun, then." He patted the stock of the carbine beside the seat. "What comes first?"

"Some clothes for you. When I saw you in the cemetery yesterday, I thought you were there to read a service! Do you have money with you?" she asked. "I can't cash a Missouri check."

"Don't worry about us Missourians. We all carry bank holdup money."

Erect on the seat, Frances drove south into the business district. A skinny mouse-colored dog wandered before the buggy, and the gray horse snorted and shied. Exasperated, Frances shook the reins. "You old fool, Granite!" Henry smiled. The horse was responding to the anxiety he felt coming down the leathers.

At a drugstore, Frances bought some powders she said might make him look less like a heathen Chinese. At a meat market she bought a ham, and then they started for a clothing store. He noticed that as they walked, not a single woman looked at her; nor did she acknowledge a single one of them. The women gave him quick, avid glances, eager to have a look at Frances's gunman friend. She wore a dark, full skirt that looked to him like a Spanish dancer's, with a white waist with lacy inserts. "My Lord, she has class!" he thought. "She'd look like a dancer if she were dressed for spring cleaning."

The men tipped their hats to Frances, except those with their wives; and all the men grinned at Henry. Several said, "Howdy, Henry!"

An older man blocked his way and offered his hand. "Knew your father, Logan! He was a fire-eating Irishman if I ever saw one! You've got a good start, yourself."

"*I hope not,*" thought Henry.

A woman whom Frances called Mrs. Murfree showed them a double- breasted shirt Henry liked, but it was a dollar-fifty, and Frances shuddered. Without expression, Mrs. Murfee showed them a denim jacket he fancied, but it was three dollars, a price Frances rejected by rolling her eyes heavenward. Mrs. Murfree's lips tightened like a purse; she looked like almost any unhappy woman Henry had seen at home, thin-lipped, powdery, and flaccid in a sacklike dress. She wore rimless glasses.

They went to another store, and a small, precise little man named Woolley showed Henry some hats. He was taken by the first one he set on his head, a Pine Ridge sombrero the color of nutria belly. The price was five dollars. In Kansas City this would have been high, but he didn't know about Nogales.

"Mr. Woolley," Frances exclaimed, "that is purely awful! A John B. Stetson wouldn't cost more than four dollars!"

"Really, Mrs. Parrish? Why don't you try the Bazaar? They have . . . cheaper goods."

Henry studied the man and his smirk. Then he removed the hat and suddenly, with a yell, pulled it down on Woolley's head; it came below his ears, blinding him, and Frances began to giggle. Sputtering, Woolley tried to lift it, but Henry pulled it down to his nose.

"No, don't take it off, Woolley — model it for me. What do you think, Frances? Is that real rabbit-fur felt?"

Frances crossed her arms, put her finger over her lips, and considered. "Heavens, I don't know what it is — I never heard of the brand."

"Well, Woolley seems to be a real rabbit, so it's possible."

Frances laughed. She said: "You mustn't be angry, Mr. Woolley — he's just funning you. I'll tell you what, Henry. Save your money. My husband has a dozen hats. In fact, you can choose a whole outfit from his closet. You're about his size. It'll be like having a husband again."

She took his arm as they left the store.

She let him hand her up into the buggy seat, smiling and a bit flushed. Henry climbed beside her and looked her full in the face. But she touched his nose with her fingertip and said, "Not to draw conclusions, Mr. Logan. That was just to start a new rumor and drive everyone wild."

She turned the buggy around for the trip north. Then she exclaimed: "Pshaw! I almost forgot — a mandolin pick."

"What for?"

"Well, I don't pick my teeth with them — I play the mandolin. Why don't you wait here while I run into the music store?"

When she emerged, the sun was nearly overhead and she had said it was twelve miles to Spider Ranch. As they neared Gorman's stable, he remembered something and dug out the stableman's love letter.

"You've got some mail."

"I have?" Frances took the smudged envelope. "Where'd you find this?"

"Read it."

Frances tied the reins and withdrew the neatly written page. As soon as she began to read, she moaned and gave him a glance of distress. She pretended to weep. Then, biting her lip, she finished the letter. For a few moments she stared down the road.

"Did you read this?" she asked.

"Read it? I wrote it. Budge's words, though. I'm sorry, but he insisted."

Rubbing her brow, she gazed at the stable. In the shade of a sidewall, wearing a leather apron, the big hairy creature called Budge was shoeing another hairy animal.

"Do you mind riding ahead a little way?" she asked. "I'll catch up with you."

Chapter Thirteen

Looking like Atlas in overalls, Budge Gorman charged from the barn as Frances stopped the buggy in the yard. His furred arms were raised to steady a sack of grain he carried on each shoulder. He wore a wild grin and was shouting, "Git moving there, Frances! Shove them boxes out of my way!"

"Budge — please!" Frances raised one hand to block the man's rush to the bed of the wagon. "Listen to me! *Stop it!*"

Budge dumped one sack atop a box of town purchases, and the buggy rocked; she managed to save a hamper in which she had packed a lunch, just as the other landed and the buggy lurched again.

Unburdened now, both his arms were reaching for her. She moaned realizing she was suddenly in a hopeless situation only a madman could have created.

141

"Git down here, woman!" he roared. "We're gonna dance!"

"I *can't!* I don't — I —"

"Sure you can." He grabbed at her.

"I don't know how!"

"I'll teach you! Come on. 'And swing that darling little maid, / She's only ninety in the shade.'"

She tried to elude him, but the wild stableman caught her wrists and swung her to the ground. Clutching her about the waist; he whirled her around and around, laughing.

"'Honor your partner!'" He bowed. Feeling ridiculous, Frances curtsied to him.

"Budge, you don't understand! I'm a married woman! If my husband saw us —"

"You just think you're married, Frances! But okay, we'll dance in the barn — dance all day and dance all night!"

He dragged her into the barn and commenced a step that made her think of a Greek folk dance, his arms raised for balance, his boots rhythmically kicking to this side and that. When she attempted to run back to the buggy, he seized her, tipping his face up to howl like a wolf, and spun her into a new pattern.

"'Old maids to the right! Young bucks to —'"

Frances tried to follow his steps, but they bumped and tangled and Budge guffawed and whirled her like a doll. He stamped, raising dust, and shouted the calls.

"Budge, *please!*"

"'Now, ladies swing in, and gents swing out —'"

Frances tried another move, going limp and pretending to faint, and Budge had his hands full keeping her from collapsing on the floor. He propped her against a wall of hay bales and peered into her face. "What's wrong, here, Frances?"

Frances waved her hand weakly. "I'm a little faint — if I could have a drink of water . . ."

"Wait here."

As soon as he turned away, she started for the door but tripped over her skirts. Budge turned back, saw what she was up to, and caught her again.

"What'samatter with you, woman? Didn't you read my letter?"

"Yes, I did. I certainly did. But, if Richard — I'm married, Budge, I'm *married!* And I don't need any more gossip."

The stableman admonished her with a finger under her nose. "Don't you realize yet that he ain't a-coming back? He's dead! Prob'ly laying under the dirt somewheres in Mexico. So you better grab another man whilst you can."

Frances shrank back. "I really couldn't marry you, anyway. I like you, very much, but I don't think we'd get along. . . ."

Budge frowned, trying to understand it, tugging at her sleeve while he pondered. "How come?"

"Because I don't love you. That's how come." She tried to smile. Curtsied. "Forgive me?"

Budge scratched his chest, his mood taking a swing, and he shook her by the arms. "Nobody else gonna marry you, Frances. You best understand that right now!"

She looked past him. In the sunlight, Granite was sleepily watching the action in the barn. In no way was he going to be part of her rescue or escape. If she got out of this, it would be her mouth that saved her.

"Yes," she said coolly, "I do understand that. But I don't want to marry anyone, ever again. And of course it would be illegal, until my husband is declared dead."

Budge pulled his hat down to the bridge of his nose and tilted his head back to stare at her, his pallid face slick with sweat. He began to wriggle his shoulders.

"You Wingards think you're so fine," he said with a smirk. "Your la-di-da papa with a chin beard like a goat. You and your fancy college ways." He made his hands dangle from the wrists and wriggled his torso in what was evidently meant to mimic a college person.

"I don't think I'm better than you," she said earnestly. "You're a good man. But you see —"

"Then how would you like to pay this good man for some of the feed your husband bought from me?" Budge yelled, pushing his face close to hers.

"I would like to, very much. As soon as —"

"And the horse he bought from me. He only paid half what he promised. Do you want to pay me the other half, college lady?"

Frances remembered the beautiful, utterly worthless chestnut Richard had shot in disgust. It was cut proud and tried to mount every mare on the road.

"But what?" Budge yelled.

"But nothing!"

"But he told you I'd sold him a wind sucker, didn't he?"

"No! That's not so."

"So now you're a horse trader! Now you're a horse doctor! Know all there is to know, don't you?"

Frances turned to march haughtily from the barn, but Budge's hand caught her shoulder and he hurled her back against the wall of hay bales lining the aisle. Suddenly she began to weep — hopelessly, in exhaustion and fright. Why had Henry not known what would happen? Why had he let her do it?

"Help!" she cried. In her ears it sounded like a child's whimper.

Budge reached above her head and yanked something from the wall of hay. Some dried straw fell into her hair. He shook the thing in her face, his lips bared and his eyes wide. It was a hay hook with a single gleaming tine like a steel fang. Frances screamed.

Budge twisted the hook and caught the top button of her shirt waist. He yanked it off. The polished point traced down her flesh to the hollow of her breast, and he snapped off another button. Then another fell, and he pulled her bodice open and looked at her lace chemise. With the hay hook he tore the lace and touched her breast with the steel.

Frances ran, stumbling, holding her skirts high.

She heard him a stride behind her as she reached the buggy. She collapsed against the leather seat, her head dropping forward.

She heard Budge sob with the effort of swinging the hook, heard it thud home but felt no pain. There was a second groan of effort, a sound of tearing fabric, but still there was no sensation. She turned her head a little and saw the steel flash as it ripped into a sack of grain inches from her shoulder. Again and again it tore through the burlap, as the grain spilled into the bed of the buggy.

Then Budge made a hoarse shout, and ran. She heard him stamping through the barn. In the silent morning, she heard her horse snorting and stamping and realized the buggy was being pulled out from under her.

Without looking back, she climbed into the buggy and let the big gray horse run.

Chapter Fourteen

The red dun was eager to travel, and Henry loped it for a minute or two, which carried him around a clump of mesquite at a turn. Then he jogged on at an easy traveling pace. He passed the last little adobe jacal and cornfield. He would have enjoyed riding all the way, but at a giant oak beside the road he dismounted and sat in the shade with his back against the trunk, wishing for one of the Frontera Hotel's cold steam beers.

He felt a touch feverish and remembered he had forgotten his quinine again.

He was carrying his old '95 gun on the saddle, and he went and got it out of its case and fooled with it, rubbing away some dust with his bandanna. A woodpecker was making a racket in the tree. He lay on his back to spot it, aimed, and made a popping sound. The bird flew.

"Don't know much about camouflage, do

you?" Henry called after it. "Head like a New Hampshire apple."

He was asleep when the crisp iron sound of buggy wheels came through the warm air. And for sure the horse was running!

Henry drove, slumped forward on a leather cushion beside the woman, wondering what, if anything, she was going to tell him about Budge. Three mysterious sacks of grain sprawled in the bed behind the seat, ripped open and with dull white grain spilling out. Frances had not yet explained, and she was in a dreadful state of nerves.

Her dress seemed to be torn, also, and every now and then she would reach up and pull the bodice together. And she would shiver, then take two or three deep sighs.

"What's wrong, Frances?" he asked finally.

"You should have stayed with me!" she charged.

He looked into her face. "Hey, that's what I thought, too. But you expressly told me —"

"I know. I'm sorry. He wanted to dance."

"Dance?" Henry laughed. "What for?"

"Celebrating our betrothal. I was so frightened! I thought he was going to kill me with a hay hook. But he finally attacked the grain sacks instead. . . ."

Henry tugged on the leathers. "I'm going

back," he said. "Evidently he didn't get the point I was making last night at the *Globe*. Keep driving — I'll take the horse."

"Don't leave me! We're going home, Henry. He'd attack you and you'd have to kill him to stop him."

It was true.

Whereas if he let Gorman get drunk tonight and pick a fight with someone else, the other man would kill him. Or the stablemen would kill him and be hung later.

Humming, he let the horse out again, kicking one leg over the side rail, trying to feel cocksure. (Captain Logan's boy strutting around with his little rifle, mimicking his daddy at Fort Bowie.)

Frances shuddered again.

"Hasn't been your best year, has it?" Henry said. But why, at this moment, did he have to remember what the priest had told him?

"No, it has not."

He thought she might be weeping, but she kept her head turned away.

Halfway home they ate sandwiches she had brought, and drank warm soda. Then it was back to the grating of iron on gravel, of sunshine reflecting off the road, and scenery that didn't change much.

He was keenly aware of the fragrance of

country flowers in her hair and clothing, probably a sachet collected and dried by her; of her little feminine movements. Sometimes she would clear her throat, sigh, or move a bit; turn her head to look at something in the brush or on a hillside. She had tied a blue bandanna over her hair to protect it against the dust. Her hair was almost black, like dark, oiled latigo leather.

But another woman said this pretty little thing had murdered her husband.

Since combat, Henry was acutely interested in the nature of the cover around him. Small trees, olive-gray, grew in the wash, which consisted mostly of sandbars. Many of the mesquites, though, were as large as oaks, dark green and thorny. A man down there had better climb a tree or dig like hell if he heard a shot, or he was a dead soldier.

To the west loomed rimrocked mountains, blued by distance; from the mountains, foothills came sloping back toward the river, peculiarly shaped formations like the skeletons of fish laid out with their tails toward the river, endless small ridges angling out north and south like fish bones. A detail trying to work toward the mountains would have all these small ridges to take, crest after bloody crest. They were tawny with dry grass and only modestly timbered with oaks.

Frances pointed. "We turn at that juniper," she said. "We're almost home. That's a hackberry tree, beyond the juniper — with the mistletoe in the branches? It looks like oak, but oak resists the stuff. The tall grass is love grass — it's pretty good grazing and Mr. Parrish has a lot of it."

"Mr. Hum Parrish? I thought he was dead."

A quick glance. "My husband."

"And is this Mr. Parrish's gun?" asked Henry, pulling the ornate carbine from the saddle scabbard beside the seat. It was the Hotchkiss-Winchester, with a tubular magazine in the stock, all the metal richly engraved with scrolls and inlaid with gold. Carved into the stock was a slogan that he read aloud: *"Let 'er RIP!* That's good." He pushed the gun back.

But Frances shrugged in disdain. "Ornamentation precedes extinction," she said.

"Excuse me?"

"As Charles Darwin and my papa used to say. Certain animals — the dinosaurs, you know — became so furbished and furbelowed with protective horns and plates that they got stuck in tight places and starved. Or sank in the pond in which they'd been admiring themselves. At least the males."

Henry chuckled. "Do you think your husband is extinct, Mrs. Parrish?"

Frances pointed quickly toward a bush. "That's an Arizona cardinal! Isn't he lovely?"

Henry admired the startlingly red bird eating berries from the shrub. "Yes, but he's so ornamental, he might become extinct, mightn't he?"

"Mr. Logan, I don't know whether my husband is dead or not. That is the truth. I could not swear either way. Tomorrow I'll show you what I mean."

"*Bueno!* I came a long way to hear your opinion." Henry smiled, but she would not look at him. He waited for her to continue with some startling revelation, but instead she lapsed into small talk.

"Are you married, Mr. Logan?"

"No, ma'am."

"Do you go to church?"

"Miss Leisure asked me that, too. And the general said to be careful or his wife would ask me. I guess the answer to all you ladies is that I go to church when the fit is on me. Why do you ask?"

"I do have a reason. One last question: Do you believe everything you read in the papers?"

"Ma'am," Henry said, "I'm a full-time bachelor, a part-time Presbyterian, and I don't believe all I read in the *Arizona Globe*. Where do we go from there?"

Frances crossed her arms and pressed her small, gloved fist against her chin. "Mr. Logan," she said, "I've had to learn not to trust any one. I've had no friends in two years. I'm trying to determine whether there is the slightest chance of our becoming — well, amigos — despite the bad start in the cemetery. You saw that the women in town snubbed me, and even the men were afraid to speak — they just grin and look down. I think that a man who isn't all tangled up in morals, and hasn't a wife telling him to beware of me, and knows that printing a lie doesn't make it true, might make — might be — I'm getting lost!"

She put her hand to her brow. "I mean that such a person might be able to understand the difficulties of my position! I've prayed till God's bored with me. Has He spoken a word to help me? Lifted a finger? Not so I've noticed."

"Maybe you don't understand His language."

She threw him a wild look, tears brimming. *"And you don't understand me, either!"*

"No, but I mean to try. Indeed I do."

As her tears overflowed, he reached down to pat her hand. She caught his hand in both of hers, then clutched his arm, jammed her face against his shoulder, and began to sob.

"Sakes alive," Henry chuckled. "Who would

guess that such a beautiful lady would have anything but friends!"

She blubbered something unintelligible.

Henry drove, murmuring nonsense in a soothing voice. Frances would cry and sniffle, try to stop, and then cry some more. He recognized that her problem had been building for a long time, and she was having to let off pressure. If the Mexican woman had told Father Vargas the truth, then understanding Frances's anguish was not difficult. And even if the woman lied, some hard nuts still remained to be cracked.

Seeing a curious rock formation a hundred yards ahead, he slowed the horse. Frances looked at him and sniffled. "Is something wrong?"

"No, no. I was just seeing if your horse was limping. He's okay."

The problem with the road was that it squeezed into a formation of towering rocks, ugly snags like discolored teeth pitted with brown cavities and topped with reddish cusps. A combat detail would never consider passing through that funnel, the perfect fore-and-aft ambush. A buggy, however, had no choice but to stay on the road, for a six-foot cut bank dropped into the wash on the right, and a thicket of bluish oak brush fenced the road on the left.

And besides, the war's over, Henry! he thought. The Spaniards hadn't been there since the eighteenth century and the Indians were on the reservation.

He remembered something. Reaching into his pocket, he said cheerfully, "You know, I've heard that one place to find peace of mind is in church. And it just happens that this morning a padre across the line asked me to give you this. . . ."

As the buggy horse trotted into the gap in the rocks, he placed the rosary on her palm. "He'd like you to visit him sometime."

"Oh, Henry! Why didn't you tell me this before we left?"

"I was afraid you might do it — and come back feeling even worse. I wanted to get your story first, and we can talk it all over — try to clear it up in your mind."

"Thank you very much. You're probably right."

"You're welcome. *Great snakes!*"

He saw a puff of dust on a yellowish slant of rock almost at his right elbow, heard a bullet strike it and take off with an unnerving *whanggg!*

Terrified, the horse reared. Henry came to his feet and fought it down, yelling; he held it in and let it run on through the gap. Frances uttered a single earsplitting shriek that tore his nerves like barbed wire. Behind the buggy the red dun was snorting but standing steady. Swearing at the gray, Henry tried to bully it off the road into a thicket at the left, but it reared again. He heard another slug hit among the rocks. He yanked the whip from the socket and slashed at the horse's rump until it dropped back to its forefeet and began to pull. It crashed through the oak brush, snorting in terror; now they were safe behind the rocks.

Henry pulled the horse in, threw the whip away, and snatched at the "Let 'er Rip" carbine, but it hung up in the scabbard and he ran back and pulled his Winchester from the saddle scabbard. He worked the bolt of the gun, reassured by its oily action. One side of his mind was saying, *The Grand Army's at it again!* Or, *Somebody's trying to bluff me out,* but another was saying, *Take it seriously! — spot him and go to work. Probably Budge Gorman has gone crazy. Or Ben Ambrose is getting something off his chest. . . .*

Henry squeezed Frances's hand, peering into her face to see what he might be up against here. Would she run hysterically down the road? The pupils of her eyes were enormous; her face was chalky. But he thought she could still follow orders.

"Just stay put!" he said. "Right here. That fool's trying to scare you. Or the Grand Army's up to some nonsense — kind of a chivaree."

She nodded, swallowed, sagged back onto the leather pillow, and began to shiver. Still nodding. Still shivering.

Chapter Fifteen

Juggling the rifle in his hands, Henry considered the huge castellated rock between the buggy and the shooter. Scrub oak filled one of the gaps at the crest of the stained rock, where he could probably take up his observation post without much chance of becoming a target. And once in position with his fifteen-shot '95 gun, he could lay down some intimidating fire. Before leaving Allie's, he had dropped a handful of shells in his coat pocket.

After a switchbacking climb through gnarled trees and a tangle of manzanita, he crawled into the thicket at the top. From here he could see the ridge to the south. The range looked like about two hundred yards, and he discounted the slight wind.

Looking for signs of smoke or movement, he found a grayish haze in an oak thicket at the crest of the ridge. In his initial shock, he had paid no attention to the sound of the gunshot, but the haze drifting through the tangle of branches had come from a black-powder shell. The seamed visage of General Miles Stockard rose to grin at him, for, like many old-time shooters, the general apparently distrusted such innovations as smokeless powder.

But Stockard had blinded his shooting eye, so how could he be the hunter? And surely he had better sense than this.

He decided that only an idiot like Budge Gorman would commit such folly. Yet, to be fair to Gorman, there was still another field-grade fool in town: Ben Ambrose. The editor wore his ego like a Congressional Medal, and Henry had certainly dented it a bit. But had he the guts to use a rifle to purge himself of his shame at letting a Kansas City gunsmith waltz out of town with a smile on his face and a pretty woman on his arm? Why not?

In his blind he waited, while in his own covert, the shooter counted the seconds.

Henry yearned to yank out his bandanna and wipe his face, but could not risk the movement. Sweat tickled his ears. Either the sun was growing hotter, or his fever was rising. Perspiration plastered his shirt to his shoulders.

He decided he had better make the first move — test the state of the man's nerves. There were boulders in the thicket, and he picked out a white facet of rock, held his breath, and locked the sights up — square peg neatly filling square hole. Then had to stop and scrub the sweat from his eyebrows. He tried again, restored the pattern of the sights, slowly closed his hand on the gun stock until the hammer fell. The gun roared and jolted his shoulder. White dust exploded in the thicket.

Finally, teeth bared, he let his intentions be known by sending ten rapid-fire shots across the swale, ripping branches and raising dust.

Frances's voice came in a scream. "Henry?"

Waiting, he slipped more shells into the tube under the hot barrel. His ears rang.

"It's all right," he called, not sure she could hear him. "I had to make sure of something."

"You can be sure I'm not going to stay here! I'm going to drive on to the ranch!"

"Wait . . ." He half raised, like a lizard, to see what was happening. "Okay! He's quit."

Dust drifted from the far side of the ridge, the military crest — the hunter was disengaging. A shod horse was clattering through the rocks, and presently he saw him in the brush alongside the road.

Driving through a grove of oaks toward the ranch, Henry greedily gulped most of the water in Frances's woolly canteen. Had

161

he brought that stuff the doctor had given him for fever? He was unsure. And Frances was so overwrought, he feared she would fly apart like a windup canary if he let her know he was going to need about fifteen hours of sleep pretty soon.

He said matter-of-factly, "I would guess that somebody was having some fun at your expense, Frances. Maybe Ambrose, maybe Budge. I don't think he'll be back."

"Or that crazy old general! He and his pop-injay of a partner make me an offer every few months. Offer? Insult. With Rip dead, missing" — she glanced at him — "I suppose they think they can intimidate me."

"I'll ask around. You've got so many enemies, Frances, I hardly know where to start."

She punched his arm. "Yes, there's always a humorous side, Henry." Suddenly she pointed. "See the flagpole? We're home — that's in my yard. Crazy old fool didn't know whether he was building Fort Stockard or a ranch house."

Henry looked over the lay of the land, considering it as a military problem. The big adobe ranch house could certainly withstand a siege, especially if the Engineers had built it for a general. Stockard wouldn't feel comfortable in anything fragile, a saltbox with a widow's walk on the roof, a cottage of some sort. All along the front of the house, at the roofline, protruded round beams that looked like the mouths of cannons. The land was flat within a hundred feet of the house, with little cover for an infantry rush — mainly mesquite and cactus. That was good, of course, but the problem was a cliff that rose fifty yards north of the house. Trees softened its rusty base, but a lesser cliff reared another twenty feet above the first, with a narrow bench separating them.

A fieldpiece or automatic weapon could be placed up there and blow the ranch house to kingdom come! A spot like that should always be under guard. But instead of a sentry, what he saw — judging by the man's appearance — was a kneeling prisoner, dispiritedly tapping away with a sledgehammer, as though cracking nuts. Henry was outraged. Where the *hell* was the sentry?

Nor did he see any sign of a work detail anywhere, and as for the horses, he made out only three old nags in a corral. The rest must be pastured somewhere. He reddened with annoyance, thinking of how to phrase his report — and yet confused, aware that there was something important to say to Frances, something he knew he had better say soon or forget.

He had to struggle, in fact, to remember what it was.

"Frances," he said, "could Rip be the Hunter?"

"The Hunter? Well, I hope he wasn't hunting us. No, I don't think Richard would be the one."

"I mean, what if he sashayed down to Mexico and got himself hurt bad — or got one of those tropical fevers — went kind of crazy, you know —" And his mind stalled, addled by one of those tropical fevers.

"It doesn't seem likely," Frances said. "Not like Richard at all. He's more forthright, I think."

"Who is?"

She looked quickly at him, with an expression of amused vexation. "Richard, of course! Who else?"

"Oh — oh, I . . ." Rubbed his brow. "So you don't think he might come back here and haunt you? Has anything like this happened before?"

"Twice. Well, like stray shots. Once it hit near where Alejandro — the Mexican boy, my maid's grandson — was digging up on the cliff. Once it nicked the flagpole. The shots always sound far off."

"In that case," Henry said, "I'll take my horse and reconnoiter a little before we go into the yard. What's the trooper's name?"

"Alejandro. He's not a soldier, Henry — don't you remember? — he's my maid's grandson. He's been drilling a month for a dynamite charge. I've got to break through the cliff behind the house to bring a sweet-water line to the kitchen."

"I see," Henry said. "Why don't you wait here, ma'am? Got some mares, haven't you? My horse wants to meet them. I call him Sniff — got a hell of a nose."

As he rode away, carbine in hand, Frances called after him, alarmed, "Henry?" but he deemed the matter of the loose prisoner more crucial than the wishes of some officer's wife. . . .

When the Mexican youth saw the sorrel-haired American riding toward him on the bench, he slowly stood up. He was holding an eight-pound maul with which he had been hopelessly tapping at the bright stub of a miner's drill, driving it right into the solid heart of the bench, as though drilling for tea from China. And Henry could have laughed, knowing what would happen if he ever managed to drill a hole and set off a dynamite charge.

He looked about, and, in a ferny cleft in the second rise of red stone behind the boy, saw a small rock-and-stone dam, penning up the sweetwater Frances had spoken of. A length of wooden pipe ran from the basin into a sawed-off whiskey barrel, and in his thirst he could almost smell the water. Around the basin grew spearmint and fragrant cliff rose and some kind of tough little fern. The Spanish prisoner smiled and raised his hand. Too bad — so many of them were just children.

"*Buenas tardes, senor!*" he said.

Henry frowned at him, definitely not approving of giving prisoners the run of the camp. Looking things over, he saw a rusty blue enamel cup among the ferns, and he went to drink long and greedily, then poured water over his head, shook the drops from his hair, and put his hat on.

"*Agua dulce!*" said the prisoner. "Good for drink!"

Henry held his eyes sternly. "Where's the guard?" he said. "*Dónde es — es —?*"

Alejandro shrugged. Turning his head, he waved at Frances, who had driven the buggy into the yard. "*Bienvenidos, señora!*" he called. Henry stared down at the fort — long and low and with a flagpole before it. The barracks was about fifty feet to the right, — by oaks and hackberries.

"Carry on," Henry said to the prisoner.

He would discuss the incident in private with the sergeant of the guard — no use making trouble for him with the brass. He led his horse down the narrow trail to the yard. After arriving, he pretended to loosen the cinches, as an excuse for leaning against the horse while his eyes cleared. In his ears he heard a pounding like that of the sledgehammer on the cliff. He realized that he was sick, and tried to remember whether he had heard the bugle announcing sick call today.

Then he turned, brisk and soldierly, but swaying. Water soaked the shoulders of his shirt and his sweaty face was still beaded. A pretty black-haired woman standing beside a buggy laid a finicky eye on him as he approached — she was actually frowning! Some of these Eastern women! He paid his respects with a sweep of his black town hat. She smiled quickly but seemed puzzled.

"Is everything all right, Henry?" she asked.

"Oh, indeed, ma'am. I wonder if I might ask a favor, though? You're the captain's wife, is that correct?"

"Henry, *what* is this nonsense? I know it *looks* like a fort, but —"

"Ma'am, I'm sorry if I shouldn't have addressed you. I wanted to ask you . . . tell you . . . inform the sergeant of the guard"

— he rubbed his brow — "that I'm going on sick call."

"Merciful heavens," Frances gasped, and she turned and raised her voice: *"Josefina! Vénte! Ayudeme!"*

Chapter Sixteen

In the jungles of his delirium, Henry floundered through hissing dens of snakes and lay
sprawled facedown in muddy ditches, stung
to shouting agonies by mosquitoes and spiders. Later he lay tied on a cot and a fat old
woman placed on his back a bit of wool, which
grew and grew until he was suffocating beneath a mountain of trash.

But in moments of partial consciousness,
he knew he was sick and that the hospital
was far from the front line, that it was vastly
superior to the first-aid tent where he had
first been treated. Though perspiration soaked
him, the steaming jungle rains no longer
slashed through the tent flap, and the insects
were gone. Two nurses came and went in
his ward: an old Cuban or Spanish woman,
and an American girl who was efficient and
quick and kept the cool water and cold cloths
coming.

And one day Colonel Teddy himself entered! The other sick men shouted greetings, but Roosevelt patted Henry's brow and said, "Don't cheer, boys — the poor fellow is dying." And he exhibited a copy of Henry's own book, *The Law of the Gun,* which was marked in a dozen places.

One night Henry heard his platoon leader screaming for help, and the two nurses together could scarcely keep him from going to cut him out of the barbed wire in which he was being crucified.

Then one night he woke and was conscious of a cool and peaceful stillness in a long dusky room. He had been carried to a small barracks. The structure was low-ceilinged and snug, with eight cots, all unmade except for his own, and one other where a black-haired trooper slept. A small lamp burned near the other trooper's cot. A cross was fixed to the white plaster wall, and brown glass bottles rested on a nightstand. Henry muttered and tried to sit up. He called, hoarsely, "Hey soldier!"

The other man raised his head and looked at him. Henry wanted suddenly to go over and have a drink with the man and swap war stories; but as soon as he swung his legs over the side of the cot, the trooper pulled on a blue robe with a white collar and hurried down the aisle to him. But there was something very odd about this soldier, who had unbelievably effeminate features and spoke in a girlish voice.

"Henry?" he said. "Do you need something?"

Embarrassed, Henry muttered, "Neh' min', fella. Thought we might have a couple of drinks."

Nevertheless, the girlish soldier helped him drink some water and gave him some medicine, then bathed his chest and back with alcohol, which brought his temperature down. Since there was no one to see, he submitted to these procedures, wondering at the funny chap's being in the Army. His personal opinion had always been that such men were usually not bad types at all.

The next time he opened his eyes, his head was clear and he knew he was not in Cuba after all. Wherever he was, an old Mexican lady sat near his cot, sewing. She was dressed in black. He tried to speak, and she rose quickly and hurried away.

While he waited, he looked over the enlisted men's quarters. A bone-deep fatigue kept him lying there perfectly content, grateful to be alive, understanding now that he had been very sick, had survived, and that his body was beginning to rebuild itself. He doubled the pillow under his head so that he could look around and see where he was.

His cot was in a long white-walled room in what looked like a very well-appointed bunkhouse. On wall pegs hung items that appeared to be cowboys' gear — chaps, coils of rope, leather jackets, spurs, quirts, and bright Mexican and Indian blankets. His eye was caught by what looked like an ivory-gripped single-action Army pistol. In the aisle was a little iron stove with a box of mesquite roots beside it.

The ceiling was of square-hewn cottonwood beams supporting a herringbone pattern of willow wands. Suddenly he remembered arriving at a ranch with the woman. He must have given her quite a time! In Cuba he had helped control the antics of malaria victims, and they could be crazy as bedbugs. He peered through a window and saw brittle, small-leafed Arizona shrubbery and a reddish, layered rimrock cliff. He perceived the upper body of a black-haired youth and heard a hammer clinking on metal.

In a few minutes Frances Parrish hurried in, carrying a cup of coffee. Her dark hair was pinned atop her head, and she wore a long white cotton dress. She set the tray on the cot beside him and sighed.

"Oh, Henry!" she said. "What a scare you gave us! Are you hungry?"

"Starved!" He waved his arm. "What kind of a bunkhouse is this?"

"It's General Stockard's idea of one. My husband used to call it the enlisted men's quarters. It's what the Corps of Engineers produced when Stockard told them to build him a bunkhouse. The ranch house has rifle loops in the roof parapets and a pantry big enough to feed a whole Army during a siege." Frances placed the coffee on his nightstand.

"Lots of cattle?" Henry said.

"Not a single cow! After he was ready to stock the ranch, his partner lost it in a gambling game. As I'm sure you know. But all he actually lost was the land — the Army built him the house and so forth. Called it a 'camp,' and then decommissioned it as soon as it was finished. Camp Logan, as a matter of fact — I'd forgotten! After your famous father."

Henry said, "He never told me. . . ."

"He was a hero in this part of the country. You can be proud. He never lost a payroll until — I'm sorry, we don't need to talk about that."

"Oh, I know about that. He died when he lost that one. But I'll tell you something, Frances . . ."

But then he began chuckling, and told her nothing. She studied him for a while, finally patted his cheek. "Josefina's making you some breakfast. After a while I'll bring you something to read, too."

"I'm sorry to be on your hands. I'll be all right in a couple of hours."

"Couple of hours? Three days at best. For a while you're going to rest and read."

"Read what? *Frank Leslie's Magazine?*"

"Papers of Richard's. Maybe you can fathom them. I can't."

After a Mexican breakfast of refried beans, tacos, eggs, and a tropical fruit he'd first eaten in Cuba, he dozed. When he woke, he saw a couple of articles resting on a chair pulled up where he could reach them. One was a wooden box with the stenciled words: BALL AMMUNITION CAL. 38-40.

So the general's hand still lay subtly upon the ranch. In the box, however, were canceled checks, papers, and a few letterpress copies of correspondence. But these were in Spanish, signed by Francisca Wingard de Parrish and addressed to the Gobernador de Sonora and the alcaldes of several towns of Sonora. But why tell him about it?

The canceled checks were also signed by Frances. For supplies according to the memo lines, things like hay and grain, tools and food. Finally he organized a small sheaf of onionskin forms with the letterhead of the United States Government Assay Office, in Oro Blanco, Ar-

izona Territory. They were made out to Richard I. Parrish and referred to having received
so many ounces of silver. The dollar value of
these silver sales were always the same — one
hundred twenty-five dollars — which happened to be the amount of Rip's monthly trust
checks.

Richard, Henry thought, *what were you up
to, you rascal?*

The enigma deepened when he examined
the last item in the box: a stained rawhide
sack tied with a thong. He shook it and it
jingled darkly like a collection of nuts and
bolts. After a frustrating battle with a har-
dened leather knot, he opened the sack and
peered inside.

It was fill of silver pesos.

As a guess, he would say about two hundred
and fifty of them — or a hundred and twenty-
five dollars' worth.

He lay back, chuckling. Richard liked a mystery, he suspected. He was digging silver
somewhere, selling it to the U.S. Assay Office,
cashing the checks at the bank for silver pesos.
. . . And then what?

For some reason he looked at the Colt hanging on the wall. He gathered his strength and
shuffled across the aisle and took it from the
peg where it hung. Sitting cross-legged on the
cot, he looked it over. It was a common sin-

gle-action Army pistol, 1872 model, but the nickel-steel barrel and frame were engraved from front sight to butt plate, and the engraver's vinelike tracings were filled with gold and silver. Rip's motto was written in silver on the ivory grips: Let 'er RIP! As a last unique touch, a tiny square-cut ruby was set into the front sight.

Looking out the window, he saw the Mexican boy carrying a couple of water buckets down the cliffside trail, and he laid the ruby on his black head and squinted. The stone filled the rear sight with red light. He lowered it, turned it, squinted at both sides of the gun. Beautiful! — but absolutely the most tasteless thing he had ever seen. And one other curious facter made him frown, some small flaw in logic. Something wrong here, Rip!

Suddenly he sniffed the barrel. And there was the answer: The weapon had been put away dirty when it was fired last. A man who had spent a fortune on this gun had left the black-powder filth to corrode the barrel.

He flicked open the ejection gate and checked the loads of the cylinder. All six chambers were filled, and he punched the heavy cartridges out onto the blanket one by one and picked up the single spent shell.

He looked at it, wondering where its lead slug was now. Trying to understand that exhausted him, and he yawned, lay back, and fell asleep.

When he woke, he found a washroom at the end of the room, with a commode, wash-basin, and mirror, and he got razor and soap, comb and clippers, from his valise and pre-pared for a painful shave with cold water. But the Mexican woman appeared with hot water just in time to save him.

Afterward he splashed on some of Rip's bay rum, tamed his sorrel hair with his hair tonic, and looked for clean clothes. On hooks under a wall shelf hung a white silk shirt, a work shirt, a dandy's trousers with a fine black-and-white stripe, jeans, and some Wellington boots.

He pulled them on. The dandy's outfit was almost a perfect fit. Every item was from a store in San Francisco.

As he admired himself in the mirror, Frances's voice called from the far end of the room. *"Que guapo tu eres!"* He saw her coming down the aisle with another tray. Henry hur-ried to take it from her, sniffing the cinnamon toast, hot chocolate, and spicy scrambled eggs.

She sniffed, too. "My, I do love the smell of bay rum! I'm glad you found it — it's really the only thing I miss about Richard."

She smoothed her skirts and sat on a cot and watched him devour the food. He kept glancing at her, grinning, admiring. Lord, Lord, he thought, no wonder Rip had to have her! The exotic dark eyes, the rich lips and thin cheeks — she was a collector's item herself, a presentation model, a miser's pride! Signed and gold-inlaid and with a ruby in her front sight.

"Papa would have been impressed by you, Henry," she said.

"How so?"

"He had a special interest in the sons of outstanding men. So many of them are either rascals or rattlebrains. The rascals go to jail, and the rattlebrains sink without a trace, drowned by the weight of their fathers' medals. Papa's phrase. Your father was apparently a fine officer."

"And I'm a rascal or a rattlebrain?"

"Papa would have known at once. I'll have to wait and find out: But you're no rattlebrain."

Henry grinned and went on eating. Frances interrupted his feasting by filling a tumbler with water and handing it to him with a pink pill. "Take this — it's best taken with food."

Henry put it on his tongue and tossed it back with a big slug of water — and choked and spat it all on the floor! Salt water! Frances exclaimed and took the glass from him.

"I'm *so* sorry! How awful — I filled the pitcher from the sink pump instead of the water bucket. Forgive me."

Henry rinsed his mouth with coffee. "What's the difference?"

"The pump draws from the alkali spring in the yard — we use it for laundry and cleaning, but it's not fit to drink. I'll get you a fresh pitcher."

"Wait. . . . The drinking water is what Alejandro carries down the trail all the time?"

"Yes. There's a wonderful spring up there. But the cliff —"

"And you plan to blow that rocky ledge off and bring a pipe down the cliff?" When she nodded, he laughed. "Praise God, Frances! A fire-cracker would have brought the whole cliff down on the house. You can see the cracks in it from here."

"For heaven's sake! Then what —"

"I picked up some good medicine for rock breaking from an Indian scout when we lived at Fort Bowie. You'll have sweetwater in the kitchen tomorrow. Bring me one of those owl feathers Rip keeps in the ribbons of his hats. And take one to Alejandro. And tell him this: Build a big fire right where he's been drilling. Line up four buckets of water and keep the fire going for

179

two hours: Then throw the water on the fire, fast."

"And put it out?"

"And stand back. I'll get up there later in the day and see how he's doing."

Chapter Seventeen

From experience, Henry knew that his system would require about three days to trap and skin out all the malaria alligators still cruising his veins. Then he would suddenly be as good as ever. Until next time.

Despite Frances's orders, he climbed the brushy trail to the bench. He found Alejandro piling dead mesquite branches, brittle and gray as old bones, onto a fire he had built at the spot where lately he had been drilling. When he saw Henry, he smiled and removed his straw hat and said something in Spanish. Henry gave him the Latin *abrazo* he had seen men using in Nogales, and then set to work explaining that he wanted four or five buckets brought up from the yard. Bring a rake and a pickax, too, he mimed.

Alejandro took off. He was *muy listo,* Frances had said — very willing.

Waiting, Henry inspected the stone rampart

he had to breach to get water across it. Seemed a pity to shatter it, it was so pretty, salmon-pink and gray and with embedded nuggets of mica resembling dice. At its lowest point, the ledge was about four feet higher than the water source. Maybe a wall could be constructed across the narrow fissure where the spring bubbled from the upper cliff, creating a dam, but there were so many cracks in the rock that filling the dam would be impossible. The little existing rock-and-cement wall would have to suffice to collect water and channel it into a pipe.

And since water traditionally refused to run uphill, the rampart must fall.

Henry fed the fire and Alejandro worked at filling the buckets he had brought. Then Henry lay on his back and let the sun warm him, a smile of contentment on his face. Ideas about Rip and his silver obsession were shifting around in his mind like trout in a pool. . . .

Suddenly the ringing of a triangle startled him. He had been asleep. He looked around, trying to comprehend where he was. Alejandro bent close to him and said: *"Lonche, señor!"*

Henry stretched. Then he signed that he wanted all the fire and frosty-red cools raked away. After the stone was cleared, so hot it glowed pink, Henry picked up a bucket, had the boy do the same, and they doused the rock. There was a single loud crack, then an angry hiss, and dirty steam erupted from seams in the rock. Boiling water bubbled in a small basin in the stone.

Henry took the pickax and worked it into a steaming crack. He pried out a long thin splinter of rock and dragged it aside, opening a deeper vein. The next assault of fire would work into that one, again the cold water would cause an explosion, and in a day or two Frances's *agua dulce* would be at her kitchen door.

Apache dynamite.

And with luck that foul alkali water would never cross his lips again.

Now that he was back on his feet, Frances showed him through the house. The Engineers with their hairy ears had done themselves proud in creating Camp Logan. No wonder Stockard wanted it back.

The parlor was a thirty-foot expanse of red tile floor and beamed ceiling like a hunting lodge, with a pueblo-style fireplace and small windows in deep adobe walls. Indian blankets brightened the walls, pots and *ollas* rested on shelves, and corn grinders were used as doorstops. There was a small pedal organ and a huge fumed-oak sideboard. On one wall was a map of Santa Cruz County.

Frances hesitated, then let him glance into her bedroom, trim, white-walled, and fragrant with the sachet he now associated with her. A mandolin lay on a chest of drawers, and Rip Parrish's overdecorated carbine leaned against the wall beside the bed. There were cattails and peacock feathers in a vase, photographs on the walls. He decided to please her by closely examining the photos of her father and asking some questions about him. In return, he got an encyclopedia of information as well as a couple of quotations from Tennyson.

Turning to leave, he decided that the room was so orderly, it might be a sort of refuge for someone whose life was a den of snakes. *And this goes here, and that goes there, there you have it!* In perfect order, unlike someone's mind.

As the days passed, his strength came back like a pasture greening up. Working under the sun was good medicine, and helping Alejandro conquer stone with two of nature's miraculous elements, fire and water, was heartening: it reinforced his belief that there was a natural solution to most of life's dilemmas.

With bare hands they were ripping a shallow

trench right through a steel-hard rampart of ancient rock.

Sometimes, while he was feeding the fire or dragging in dry fuel he would hear Frances plucking her mandolin, the music floating through an open window. Was she healing her desperate hurts, as his body was curing his? Realizing he must soon ask her about Father Vargas's story, he sighed.

Late in the afternoon of the fourth day, he and the Mexican boy chipped the last bits of granite from the stone dike, cleared away all the debris, and the water began to trickle down the cliff.

Camp Logan now had sweet springwater to drink.

They rode from the ranch yard an hour after dawn the next morning. Leading a pack mule heaped with gear for a night in the open, Henry felt strong and cheerful, drawing the thin cold air into his lungs and feeling his muscles tingle with energy. He wore some of Rip Parrish's clothing, a double-breasted shirt, jeans, a denim jacket. In the hatband of Rip's John B. Stetson 5X beaver, he wore the owl feather.

Brown as old buckskin, the range began to break up into canyons divided by low ridges. Frances followed a cow trail he could scarcely see, riding confidently across bald ridges and up brushy canyons in a southwesterly direction.

Once, from a ridge, Henry's eye was caught by a flash on a hillside to the south. He pulled his old brass spyglass from its case and focused on the spot where it shone, then relaxed and put the scope away. He had merely seen the sun flashing on a cow's horns.

The episode brought something to mind.

"Where are your cattle?" he asked. "I take it you're resting this pasture?"

"My cattle," said Frances, "are in some gambler's pocket, as far as I know. Richard went on a lot of buying trips, but somehow never brought any home. I believe there are forty or fifty Mexican steers out there somewhere. All horn, hoof, and hide."

At high noon, in the shade of a blackjack oak, they devoured some of the big wheat-flour tortillas of Sonora, along with cold beans, Mexican coffee cakes, and cold coffee. Then they rested a few minutes, and Frances reminded Henry to take his quinine. With no whiskey to wash it down, he groaned, beat his breast, and panted as it filled his system with an unendurable bitterness. Frances laughed, lying back against a boulder under a hackberry tree and shooing gnats with a small branch.

"Too bad, but you have to take the stuff, Henry, or suffer the consequences."

"Did you think I'd take it for any other reason?"

She pointed into the sky with the branch. "Look! That's a golden eagle. He's on our coins, you know."

Henry found the huge bird tilting in the blue sky above a mesa. "Who told you that? That may be a golden eagle, but the one on the coins is a bald eagle."

"Then Rip lied to me. He was such a talker. He knew everything there was to know."

Henry saw a chance to make a move. "Did he know about cleaning guns?"

The branch, tracing huge white clouds, went suddenly still. "He was absolutely persnickety about it. Why?"

"Persnickety people," said Henry, lying on his side now to observe her reaction, "don't put their favorite hog legs away dirty. That Peacemaker of his was fired once and then not cleaned. That's like not changing a baby's diaper, except that talcum powder won't take pits out of steel. Why didn't he clean it?"

Frances turned also and lay facing him. The dark blue eyes searched his face. He longed to stroke her cheek and trace her lips with his fingertips. He saw her breast rise and fall to a half dozen breaths before she spoke. She said: "Don't rush me, Henry."

"Why didn't he clean it?"

"He couldn't."

"Why not?"

"It was in the cabin, with me. You see . . ."

Then her eyes squeezed shut and she turned her face away.

Henry placed his hand on her cheek and gently stroked it. "Anything you tell me," he said, "is in confidence. Consider me your priest — Father Logan. Father Logan has more secrets than a graveyard. But I have to know whether your husband is dead. People are insisting on knowing. People he owes money to."

She shook her head.

He went on: "When I know exactly what happened, then I can advise you, Panchita. By the way, what's Panchita mean?"

"Francie. Frankie."

He kissed her cheek. "I like Panchita, or even Francie, better."

"Considering what happened to Johnny, I do, too."

"And I really love Frances."

No answer.

He went on, briskly then. "So if you . . . well, think you may have killed him, then you might should stay in Sonora while I get a lawyer working on it. In fact —"

She looked at him. Henry chuckled.

"We could go to Central America and live, if things are hopeless."

"Oh, they're hopeless, all right, but what would we, I live on?"

"I think I have some money waiting for me down there. In Costa Rica."

"Well — anyway, I didn't kill him!"

"Well, Catalina Cachora says you did, but who'd believe a prostitute? Not Father Logan."

Frances sat up and began tucking in her hair. "I fired the gun. I'll show you the bullet hole — and it isn't in Richard. But first we've got to get there, and I'll tell you the story when you can see what I'm talking about. I can tell you this much right now: He was digging for treasure and living with a Mexican woman. I caught him out. I didn't care — I was through with him, anyway. I just had the bad luck to — to — let's go, Henry."

His first glimpse of the church made him draw a breath of pure pleasure. He thought the narrow wash under the clear sky beautiful, and the glimpse of crumbling adobe walls on a bench above them spoke excitingly of the ancients who had built the church here in the wilderness. But he was not so charmed as to forget the Hunter, and while he looked things over with his spyglass, they held their horses and the pack mule at the edge of a foot-deep stream in the gorge that was only forty yards wide. Clear and whiskey-colored, the stream flowed silently over a bed of garnet pebbles. The afternoon was silent except for the music of a breeze in the stiff-needled little piñon trees. For such small trees, they made a powerful lot of noise. The horses put their muzzles in the stream and sucked at the water, pawing at the gravelly streambed. The cliffs reared up steeply, and the bench with the church walls loomed like the prow of a ship.

Henry used the glass then to study all the higher ground. Near the wash, volcanic towers and domes rose from the trees, looking like old rust-streaked fortifications. What interested him particularly was a bald half dome on the south side of the wash, looming hundreds of feet above the dark green trees that hid its base. Chalky and fissured, it was fringed with oak brush at the top, and halfway down he picked out a bench that looked accessible. But from here he could see no trail to the top of the dome. If a trail existed, it must be in the back. That top would be a fine lookout, though — a sniper's dream.

Frances pointed to a small grove that ran up against the base of the dome. "There's a little meadow in there," she said. "It's the delta of a side canyon. You can't see it, but someone built a rock wall across it to hold cattle in the canyon."

"And where's the so-called Lost Mine of the Padres?"

"Just beyond, the wall. I don't think you'll be impressed by it. Bats love it, though."

Henry looked things over once more, removed and replaced Rip's fine Stetson, and said, "Let's look at that church first."

"Yes." Frances sighed. "I think a prayer might be a good way to start your investigation."

Henry was awed by the scope of the ruin. He stood before it with his carbine over his shoulder, like an infantryman. Frances took shelter beneath an old pear tree in the ancient fruit orchard, Rip's carbine in her hands. Weeds and small shrubs grew on the deep mud walls of the church; nothing remained of the roof; and there were no doors. Of the windows only a dozen square openings were left intact, preserved by rotting frames and rusty iron bars. But the structure had been solid and probably beautiful. A portico still stood at the entrance, fifteen feet high, built of rock and mud and with scabs of plaster clinging to it.

He poked around the church like a sightseer, picking up fragments of broken china, thick and blue-figured shards of pottery. He found a large copper penny, black with corrosion. He saw some horse manure which, he was pleased to see, was at least a month old. Finally he decided that things on this side of the wash looked innocent enough. The most sinister indications were an impressive number of glory holes where treasure hunters had dug.

He joined Frances, and they walked through the cemetery. Among the weeds were stone markers and rotting wooden crosses. Some of the graves had sunk a foot or more, leaving shallow troughs. But one of them caught his eye. It was heaped a few inches higher than the earth around it, and the weeds that grew on it were small annuals, not tough shrubs. Someone had been buried here not too long ago. Yet the wooden marker was already rotting. He paused to study it while Frances waited.

"What do you see?" she asked.

"I was just thinking. . . . You know those assay slips of your husband's? Well, it seems to me they prove that he was finding silver out here."

"Pooh," Frances said.

"For a rich widow," Henry said, "you don't seem very interested in your buried treasure."

Frances said, "I have seen armies of poor devils march into this county with their maps, and march out barefoot. Every so often, some Tucson printer runs off a batch of treasure maps and sells them, and the poor fools go out there and dig. Richard had a dozen. All anyone ever finds are pieces of broken blue-willow plates like I saw you picking up.

"But I've seen proof" Henry said, "that Rip was finding silver."

"Proof! What proof?"

"A silver candlestick he gave Father Vargas. It's dated 1723 and looks dented enough to be the real thing."

"That's impossible! He hated churches, especially Catholic churches."

"Well," Henry said, "I saw it."

"Oh, I don't deny that. I just think he bought it somewhere in California, had a date engraved on it, dragged it behind his horse or something, and gave it to Father Vargas to buy God knows what — forgiveness? — probably for some monstrous sin I haven't heard about yet."

"You don't trust him, do you?"

"If Richard were a clerk," Frances said, "he wouldn't know the truth if it were filed under T."

Henry laughed. Her head raised haughtily, Frances went on through the cemetery to the trail to the wash. But Henry went to one knee and with his pocket knife dug at the loose earth of the recent grave. Then he dug at the earth a few feet away, and found it much harder.

He read the inscription on the wooden cross: R.I.P. VALENTINE O'BRIEN, A NATIVE OF BEDFORD, MASS. 1858-1885.

Rest in Peace, Valentine, he thought, *but I'm fearful that somebody's been digging in your resting place. Because R.I.P. spells Rip, and that was Richard's nickname, and I think if somebody were to dig here, he would find Rip Parrish lying on top of you. What a perfect place to hide a corpse! Somebody with a sense of humor has been here with a chuckle and a shovel.*

Chapter Eighteen

When he reached the edge of the bluff, Frances was already halfway down the trail. From his vantage point he studied Rip's little camp. What he could see of it looked like the lair of a hunter or trapper. Traps and ropes and branding irons hung from the limbs of a tree, and there was a small rusty sheet-iron oven. A huge stump near a fire ring had been cut into the shape of a barber chair. A small rock house was crowded so closely against the cliff that the bluff itself formed its back wall.

He raised his gaze beyond the camp to the small meadow where the side canyon emptied into the wash. Hardly fifty yards wide, the canyon was sealed by a fieldstone wall running from east to west.

From the bottom of the trail, Frances was waving at him. Henry put the '95 Winchester on his shoulder and headed down the bluff, feeling tired after the long ride, and apprehensive at the thought of what he might be about to learn from Frances.

When he reached the camp, she was already busily throwing off the diamond hitch across the pack mule's load. She let him help her but had no intention of quitting. She had energy. She also possessed beauty, played a musical instrument, and could quote poetry. What more did a ranchwoman need? A man, obviously.

"It's going to be dark in an hour," she said, "and we don't want any light here. Why don't you look at that big stump while there's enough light to see it? That's where I think Richard died."

"Oh, so you do think he's dead?"

"Yes. But I can't swear to it."

Henry dumped the big oiled canvas roll on the ground and left Frances to spread it. He led the horses and mules to the mouth of the side canyon, put them inside the stone fence, and closed the Texas gate — three strands of rusty barbed wire.

He went back and placed himself in the heart of the treasure hunter's camp. With, one foot on the seat of the massive stump, he looked around. Overhead, the shadowy branches of a blackjack oak meshed in a dense web. He tried to see the big half-dome butte he had picked out as such a fine sniper's roost when he first laid eyes on it; but the trees over-hanging the camp completely blocked it out. So if Rip Parrish had indeed died on this juniper throne, he had not been shot from the dome.

The throne had the rough elegance of Shaker furniture, made to accommodate people's bodies but not to coddle them. The stump was a full four feet thick. Someone had simply sawed a tree off about six feet from the ground, possibly for timbers for the church. Then a later woodsman had made a horizontal saw cut halfway through this tall stump, lopping it off at the comfortable height of about twenty inches. Finally the soft juniper wood had been split right down to seat height. Now there was a seat and a back. Either long usage or someone with an adz had hollowed and smoothed the back and chamfered the edge of the seat, creating a fine place to sip whiskey with friends, to look at treasure maps and swap yarns.

Frances was building a fire under the sheet-iron oven. She called, "Do you see it?"

Henry had just spotted it — a round hole about eighteen inches above the seat and dead in the center of the chair back. He pushed the tip of his ring finger into the hole. His pip knuckle was just an inch in diameter and made a fair thickness gauge for estimating calibers. The hole seemed to have been drilled by a .50 caliber slug, maybe even larger, a bullet from some freakish gun barrel like Budge Gorman's.

Right through the brisket.

Henry wouldn't mention it to the widow, but it had taken a little bone in to the chair back with it. He could feel something sharp in there. Tomorrow he would dig it out.

"So he was sitting here when he was shot?"

"Henry, I'll tell you when we get our breath. Slice me some of that ham, will you?"

Humming, Henry got to work. As a bachelor, he understood that kitchen chores did not do themselves, and he worked with skill and a deep pleasure that he and this woman were performing a rite of important domestic significance. How might it be phrased? *With this skillet, I thee troth?*

By the time they had washed the dishes, the firelight had crumbled to coals and the daylight was gone. Frances dosed him with his quinine and he put on a pantomime of distaste to make her smile. Afterward he sat on the stump, but she said quickly: "No! Don't *ever* sit there."

He knew she was ready to tell him about Rip's death now. She was rubbing her hands together as though they were cold. She stood up from the flat rock where she was sitting.

"I'm sure he died there," she said. "But I was in the cabin when I heard the shot. I'll show you. There's a candle there, if the packrats haven't eaten it."

Henry lighted his small Army lamp. Frances led him to where the cabin huddled against the bluff. She took the tin lamp and illuminated the planks of the homemade door; though thick and iron-strapped, they were beginning to rot, and there were the cuneiform marks of an ax blade. Then she pointed out a splintered hole, high up.

"That's my shot."

"I wouldn't brag about it. Couldn't even have taken his hat off."

"No. But it scared the wits out of him. So he left me alone."

"What was he doing? What was the problem? Little marital disagreement?"

Frances pushed open the door and led him into the musty-smelling cabin. Somehow the packrats had failed to fill it with rubble, and even the canvas Army cot looked clean. She found the votive candle and Henry lighted it. She sat on the bed.

"I was sitting right here praying, and he was out there chopping his way to his fair lady. He was drunk, and probably ashamed that I'd caught him out — no, I'm wrong — there was no shame in the man. So he was going to win my hand by . . . raping me. Finally, when I couldn't stand it any longer, I fired at the door with that Peacemaker you like so well."

"I didn't say I liked it, Frances. It's just purty. I like a Smith and Wesson double-action better. Were you actully afraid of him?"

"Well, what do you think?" she cried. "Sitting there like a helpless sacrificial maiden?"

"You helpless?" Henry sat down close beside her and took her hand. "You're a brave lady, and as ingenious as a crow. Tell me about that night, from shuffling the cards to who won the pot."

She told him that after the shot had driven Rip away, back to his banjo and wine bottles, she had finally fallen asleep. . . .

But she had been awakened by a shot. It was one loud crashing shot from a distance, and after it she had heard the echoes still pouring down the canyon. And, amazingly, she thought she heard a last nasal chord fom Rip's banjo! Then a cough, and a heavy, sprawling thud.

She was afraid even to look outside. If Richard had been murdered, and anyone knew she was in the cabin, then she might be killed, too!

After what she reckoned was nearly an hour, she heard another shot nearby, then scuffling sounds, gruntings like a wild pig rooting in the camp, and finally splashing noises from the creek.

And that was the end of it.

In the dawn light she looked over the camp. Sparrows were pecking about the ground and her horse was grazing near the creek, saddle still aboard but skewed to one side. From the fire hole trailed a last bit of smoke.

But of Richard there was no sign. Holding the revolver in both hands, she went to where he had been playing his banjo and sipping wine. Gouts of blood on the chair and the ground made it plain that her husband had been shot and his body carried away.

"So I just kept quiet about it." She sighed. It was almost dark now. "I didn't want to be accused of his murder, or even be involved — I just hoped it would all fade away like the dream. I cashed the checks, but I could hardly tell Mr. Manion what had happened, or he'd write Sheriff Bannock, and there I'd be again."

"Well!" Henry said cheerfully, smashing his palms together. "Let's clean out this cabin,

Frances, and fix you up a bed."

"Where will you sleep? Don't be too far away. . . ."

He was tempted to say, just to test the waters, "Why, I'll sleep right beside you," but it was no time for joking.

Frances spread her bedroll on top of the old, stale-smelling blanket. Then, as Henry prepared to depart, she looked wistfully at him. Her braids traced her bodice almost to the waist, and the shadows in her face stirred him.

"Where will you be?" she asked anxiously.

"I plan to be on the roof," he said. "The parapet is a soldier's dream. Good night, Frances."

"Duerme con la pierna suelta!"

Notched into the cliff, Henry discovered, was a sort of stone stairway to the roof. The roof itself was of the familiar Mexican construction: layers of close-laid willow wands for a ceiling; then earth; tarpaper or tar; and in this case a layer of dry leaves. He unrolled his blankets on the leaves.

Then, in the old jungle style, he lay motionless a while with all his senses turned. Overhead, the stars blazed whiter than he had ever seen them, and the Milky Way spread a glowing phosphorescent path. He tried to understand something — how Parrish could have been shot from any of the cliffs with the trees hiding him — but his mind went out of focus and he slept.

Chapter Nineteen

Shortly before daylight, his rifle slung, Henry climbed the bluff behind the house. He found a vantage point among some boulders and got comfortable. Yawning, he sat cross-legged with his rifle on his lap, sipping cold coffee from a canteen and watching the dawn come with shades of lilac and pink. But beneath the lovely feminine tones of the sunrise, the landscape emerged like some old religious picture of hell. Crazy volcanic horns and ribs erupted from the land, and little peaks rose like fangs. Among them stood black buttes naked as stumps. A visiting hell-fire preacher might accept this as a vision of Hades and go home to describe devils taking their ease beside rivers of ash in dead canyons, while starving sinners sifted the clinkers for morsels. . . .

He started, realized he was dozing. *Wake up, Henry!* he thought. *You haven't gone to hell yet, but you will if you let the Hunter catch you napping.*

Putting his hunting scope to his eye, he searched for the dust or smoke of travelers, but saw nothing to think twice about and craned forward to scrutinize the camp below him. He saw a flake of fire, and smoke rising through the trees: Frances was up and doing the chores.

He could see the executioner's chair, and ran his eye from it to the top of the half-dome, towering a hundred feet higher even than the bluff where he sat. A bullet, though allowing for a high, arching trajectory, would have to tear through the foliage of the oaks, and certainly be deflected. Nor could Rip have been seen on the stump! So Frances was clearly wrong about the season of the killing. The trees must have been bare, so that the bullet would have had some chance of threading the needle through the bare top branches.

But that spelled winter — not spring.

Down below, he saw Frances looking for him, Rip's carbine in her hands. With her black hair hanging, and in her leather skirt, she looked like an Indian woman. He whistled and she looked up and waved, and wondering how you accused a woman you loved of lying about a murder, he started down the bluff.

While Frances cooked a line rider's breakfast, Henry wandered about the camp, counting Rip's wine and whiskey bottles. The wine was local, but the whiskey was a national brand that made him thirsty. He might have been an interesting man to know, an amusing friend. A friend for a man, that was, not for a woman. He had heard that Arizona was hard on women and horses. Rip evidently loved to sit around drinkin', pickin', and singin', to make a show — drink whiskey in cemeteries and make friends with beautiful women. Well, the man had had impeccable taste there.

And the man loved to gamble, of course.

What was the gamble he was making out here? Was there actually free silver in that mine? Because there was no ore-pulverizing equipment, none of the other enormous paraphernalia of ore reduction.

Yet he was banking pure silver.

Frances called to him. Sitting on empty dynamite crates, they ate salty ham between slabs of sourdough bread and drank strong coffee. Without discussing it, both avoided the executioner's chair. Frances, looking drawn, had pinned her hair up and pulled on a Mexican blouse with red embroidery. But her hair kept straggling down, and she seemed nervous, biting her lip and brushing at wisps of hair. Her face was thinner and there were blue smudges under her eyes. She was losing weight, and she'd had none to spare. He wished he could put her to bed for a week and take care of her — return the favor.

She managed to smile at him as he refilled her cup. "You look like a beat-up old cowboy," she said. "Do you feel feverish?"

"Ma'am, I am at my malarial best."

"Have you taken your quinine?"

"Hey, I was just going to."

He went through the quinine pantomime while she giggled, and he wished again for a little whiskey.

Afterward he put the rifle to his shoulder and used the scope to reconnoiter the brushy delta of the side canyon, the rock wall that enclosed it, and the bluff. But when he tried to aim at the dome atop the bluff, he saw nothing but a blur of green.

"Can't be done." He sighed.

"What can't?"

"If Rip were sitting on that there stump, Frances, the Hunter couldn't have hit him from anywhere but right here. Where I'm sitting — or you. Because look up — can you see the dome?"

"Of course not. I'll take you up there after breakfast, Henry. You can see the whole county — there's an Indian ruin, a lookout or something. Without the leaves on the oaks, you'd have a perfect shot at the stump! If you can picture the trees bare, and Richard sitting there . . .

"When the leaves are on the ground," Henry agreed, "there'd be a good chance. But I think you said April."

Frances looked at him blankly, then smiled. "Oh, my, I see your problem now! You're looking at the trees like a Missourian. But these are good old Arizona black oaks, and for some strange reason the leaves hang on all winter. And then, first thing in March, they drop! In April the branches are still bare. Richard was killed in April, two weeks before the oaks greened up."

Henry stretched and said, "I can't tell you how glad I am to hear that. If you told me a little green man came out of the mine and shot him, I would make every effort to believe you. I would sift the county for little green men. But who else would believe you? Whispering George Bannock? Ben Ambrose? No, ma'am — before this news hits the sidewalks of Nogales, we've got to cook up a believable story."

She looked at him archly. "'Cook up'? Isn't that something dishonest lawyers do?"

Henry laughed. "Well, dishonest lawyers and honest gunsmiths."

"I really am not lying, Henry," she said.

"And I'm not lying when I say I'm going

to figure out how that shot was made. It's all in the numbers, Frances. The Hunter knew his tables. Damned genius," he said. "One shot? Impossible! But he did it."

"What numbers?"

He considered how to simplify a very complex equation. He began with descriptive motions of his hands.

"Numbers like how far the bullet has to carry. And how high, in order to clear the trees. Bullets don't travel flat, you know — they climb, *a lot*, lose speed, and drop. The tables will tell me how high a trajectory. Five or six feet, at least. And the slug's got to start fast, reach just the right elevation, and then dive like a red-tailed hawk — not fall like a stone.

"Sometimes the figures shock you! They say, Henry, you'd need a cartridge they don't make! Savage doesn't make it, Stevens doesn't make it, Marlin doesn't. A shell called an H and H Magnum might be close. The solution lies in using exactly so much powder and a precise amount of lead. For the Hunter, it meant that to carry the trees and come down fast would require a special shell. I don't think there's any doubt of it."

Fascinated, Frances watched his hands drawing out a slim brass tube. "Well — where could he get it, then?"

"He could make it. Take something like an old Sharps buffalo load and modify it. Start at .50 caliber and neck it down to .45. Throat it to use a couple of paper patches, for maximum spin when the bullet left the gun. But I'm still bothered," he said with a sigh.

"Why?"

"Because even with the leaves on the ground and the right load, no sniper could hit that stump the first time. He'd have to make a dozen practice shots first. He'd need a spotter, too — he couldn't take an hour's hike every time he fired. So he's got a cohort. A man down here flag-signals him where he's hitting. Bullets are dropping all over the camp, and the spotter hides behind a tree.

"Then the Hunter finally hits the chair. When he puts five or six shots in a six-inch circle, he's ready. But those ranging shots leave holes, Mrs. Parrish! And I don't see holes — only the one that, um, killed him. The slug's still in there, by the way. It didn't go through the wood. I'll dig it out later."

Frances shrugged. She was involved in all this speculation up to the eyebrows, but like most women, she hated guns. Their minds just turned off when they saw one of the nasty things.

But he persisted. "Don't you see the problem in all this shooting? It had to go on when

Rip was at the ranch! But why didn't he notice the holes when he came back? If he was them, he'd say, 'Hey, Rip! Don't you think maybe that chair isn't the healthiest place to sit?'"

Then he opened his pocket knife and carefully inspected the stained seat in the ancient stump. For the first time he noticed a long, dark stain that might be grease, but might also be blood. The chair back was a concave slab of soft silvery-gray wood. He went to work like a furniture refinisher. Scraping the juniper revealed a fine-grained pinkish heartwood with an aroma like that of a cedar chest. Tough breed of tree! he thought. Dead twenty years, maybe a hundred years old, and still aromatic.

The blade caught on something harder than juniper. He squinted, made a sound, and beckoned to Frances, who stood across the fire ring, pinning her hair up.

"What do you see?"

He stabbed at a blemish in the wood, perfectly round, about a half inch in diameter, and resembling a dowel in a piece of cabin furniture: End-grain wood instead of the long straight grain of the body of the piece.

"What is it?" she asked.

With the point of the knife he pried at the foreign wood until it loosened. After digging out some of the wood around it, he managed to extract a dowel of the same kind of wood as the chair. About three inches long, it was apparently a section cut out of a small branch.

"Practice shot," he said. "He plugged it and then smoothed it over. Stained it with coffee or something so it wouldn't be noticeable. Let's go up and see if he left me some cartridges . . ."

Frances said they would have to walk. The only way to the bench was by a trail only she and the foxes knew about. The dome rested on the flat bench like a derby hat on a table. From the front it appeared inaccessible, but she said it could be scaled from the back. Along the lofty edge of the dome ran a capstone that looked like the parapet of a castle. In fact, Frances said, it was the wall left by prehistoric people.

She led the way up a sandy path in the middle of the canyon, through tall clumps of saw-edged bear grass and oak brush to the nearly vertical west wall of the wash. The base was hidden by brush, but Frances pushed straight into a thicket and disappeared. He followed her by the moving brush and the clouds of choking dust shaken from the leaves. When he caught up with her, she was standing at arm's length from the stone wall, pointing.

"There!" she said.

All he saw was a narrow crack in the rock. "That?" he said.

"Oh, come on, Henry! You Missourians! Don't you know anything about mountains? Walk sideways, like a crab. . . ."

She slipped into the passage, disappeared, and called back, "Like that! Come on!"

Henry held his rifle over his head and squeezed into the slot. His belt buckle scraped in front and the hip pockets of Rip's Levi's dragged in back. Oh, my God, he thought. He had a native dread of tight spots. But stumbling over rubble, swearing under his breath, he scraped along. Hard freezes and ages of waterborne sand had chiseled out this narrow crack in the stone. He wouldn't call it a trail. In another thousand years it might be one.

"Henry?" she called, from far ahead.

"Hello," Henry muttered.

He struggled on, sweating and swearing, as the heat thickened and tiny stinging gnats sang about his ears. What if he became delirious again? What a place to get sick! Frances could no more drag him out of here than she could a dead steer. Why, a dead man couldn't even fall down in this place!

Then, to his relief, he saw her only a few yards ahead in a sort of chamber an arm span wide, floored with the trash of dead branches and the litter of generations of pack rats. It was the end of the trail, or the beginning, for he could see that a miniature waterfall had cut away at the solid rock until it opened a crack. Propped against the wall, a dead piñon tree made a natural ladder to the ridge above.

Frances clambered through the dry, brittle branches and Henry scrambled after her, eager to get out of the torture chamber.

He emerged onto a narrow ridge running straight back toward the wash. Barely wide enough for a path, it was swept by a breeze that the Hunter must have worried about. Winds ordinarily died at sunset, but what if —? So he might have had to make a last-minute decision on windage.

Frances stopped and faced west, her arm pointing. "We rim out there — at the black mesa. And north where — well, someplace — and you can see most of our landmarks from here." She looked at him, flushed. "I watched a sunset from here once. You can't imagine —!"

"Bet I can. Bet the Hunter watched a few sunsets, too."

They had to walk north, then, as far as they had walked south up the blind canyon, and it was rocky going, the ridge stripped down to bed-rock. Tough mountain shrubs had their iron claws in the rock, and the wind hissed through little twisted piñon trees. He had been timing the trip, and as they reached the bench he looked at his watch. Thirty-five minutes and they weren't on the cap yet.

He moved to the edge of the bench in the strong breeze. Frances watched his pleasure as he discovered the scene below. From here, the camp looked like a railroad company's advertisement for a projected town in some grim wasteland where they were selling city lots. *There* was the mine opening, *there* the stone corral; and the wash ran east and west a few hundred feet north.

But because of the trees, the shot would not have been possible from here. So if there were any evidence of what had happened, it would be up on the dome.

Frances cried, impatiently, "Come, Henry!" and headed for the southwest face of the dome. Here it had crumbled to a talus slope of boulders piled against the solid stone like gravestones dumped from above. She shaded her eyes to peer up the slope, then started nimbly up the rocks.

Henry muttered and followed her. Damned ague had left him short of energy. His ears were ringing when they reached the summit, a roughly square space forty or fifty yards across. Weeds grew everywhere, and brush, and in places the Indian walls had crumbled. They were built close to the edge of the bluff on the north and east sides, and were constructed to last.

They crossed the dome to a seven-foot wall made of flat stones. In its center was a narrow vestibule through which, he supposed, people were supposed to enter — a full-height inlet into a tiny room, with egress to the outside. Unwelcome strangers would arrive single file, to be shot or clubbed as they came.

He stepped outside. There was a path a few yards wide clinging to the wall. He peeked over the edge of the cliff — a typical lovers' leap above the meadow a few hundred feet below. Frances was already out of sight around a bend in the wall; he heard her calling. When he caught up, he found her looking at a heap of stones like a surveyor's monument, at the very edge of the cliff: Flat rocks had been dragged there and stacked a couple of feet high. At one end the stones stepped down to a ledge, forming a seat.

"I suppose that's an altar or something," Frances said.

Henry chortled. The dominoes were beginning to fit. "No, ma'am. That pile of rocks really makes an old sniper sentimental, Miss Frances."

He got in position on the seat and rested the forearm of his rifle on the ledge. It gave him an absolutely steady rest for the gun barrel. Once set, he could adjust the sights quickly and be ready to fire. Then, afer the kick, he could reload and lay the barrel back exactly where it had been. To demonstrate, he sat on the bench and looked for a target down in the meadow. He picked one of the horses, got into the marksman's position, and squinted across the iron sights. He said, "Ahh!" raised his head, looked around, and told Frances, "That's how it was done. He sat here like a schoolboy and took his tests. Went to school here and graduated that night."

"Summa cum laude," Frances murmured.

"How's that?"

"Pig Latin."

"You went to college to learn Pig Latin?" Henry's spirits soared like a hawk. He had added all the numbers, and everything tallied. At least, almost everything.

"No, but I learned to write prescriptions and play the mandolin."

"Did they teach you how to find bottlenose shells? I need one of those even more than I need Pig Latin."

Frances looked at the ground. "Would he leave any?"

"Not the practice shells. He'd be able to find and pick them up. Except maybe the ones that went over the bank. Those would be down there on the bench."

They looked around, brushing away leaves, turning flinty stones. Frances found the first shell. It had lodged in a bush a few feet below the rim — a bit risky to reach, so he had left it there. Another shell snuggled under the rock that formed his seat, out of sight. Frances retrieved the cartridge in the bush, but after looking the second one over, Henry said, "Let's leave it — let the sheriff find it."

He took a breath. "And now, one last question. We know how he did it. And I think we know why. But what I don't know is why he went to all the trouble of shooting a man from up here, with a special rifle! Why not just lay for him near the camp and knock him out of that chair?"

Frances blinked. Then she smiled. "Oh, it's like the leaves — I haven't told you all the little details. He couldn't get near that camp without Richard's knowing! Richard might have shot him first."

"Why?"

"The dog! Richard had the smartest dog in creation, according to him. It could smell a horse or a man a half mile away, or hear him a mile off. No one could ever have crept up on him. You see?"

"But what happened to the dog?"

"The Hunter shot him, too. That was the

last shot I heard, later that night, when the man came down to drag the body away."

Henry felt vastly better. As fine a job as the Hunter had done of getting the right gun, the perfect shell, and his sniper's roost, all that effort just hadn't made much sense, somehow.

But the dog explained it.

While Frances made sandwiches, Henry inspected the rusty mining equipment and peered into the mine. The machinery had been there for a coon's age, he was sure, and the meager size of the mine dump showed it had not been tunneled very far into the cliff. Using the little Army bull's-eye lamp, he explored the mine but found nothing more exciting than a mummified bat hanging against the rock wall.

If Rip Parrish had been finding silver, it must have been in the form of church artifacts and money the padres had held out on the king of Spain. He caught the horses and let them back to camp. Frances, anxious to leave, told Henry that if they left now, they would be home well before dark. She had started packing while he was exploring the mine. Henry said, "Sure," saddled the horses, adjusted the packsaddle on the mule, and decided to get it over with.

"Do you know a woman named Catalina Cachora?" he asked.

Frances, brushing her hair, looked at him oddly. The sun made the dark plaits gleam like a racehorse's hide.

"Of course. She was the woman Richard was living with. She and I said adios, all very friendly, and she rode away on her burro. Oh, wait," Frances said, frowning. Brush in hand, she gazed down the meadow. "That's funny. She went the wrong way! She couldn't have gotten out with the burro. It's a blind canyon. Yet she didn't come back — that I know of, at least."

Henry scratched his neck. "Yes — that's what she told Father Vargas. That she had to come back."

"Well, I didn't see her. I must have locked myself in the cabin by then."

"Probably. And you never came out? Just fired that one shot to scare him off?"

Frances pointed the brush at him and demanded, "What is it, Henry? What did she tell him?"

"She said she saw you cash in his chips."

"What?"

"Shoot him."

Her eyes closed, Frances clenched her fists. "That is a *lie!* It happened precisely —! What exactly did she tell him? What?"

"That she ran away from the camp but got boxed in and had to come back. And that — that she saw you shoot him and he fell out of the chair."

"She was too scared to know what she saw! She only *heard* the shot — and I suppose saw him fall. But I was barricaded inside the cabin!"

"Well . . ."

Frances threw the brush down. "That woman! I didn't even berate her! We just — Henry, there's something very odd about this. Did she tell Father Vargas this fairy tale in the confessional? Because if it was a confession, then he shouldn't even have told you."

Henry picked up the brush and fondled a plait of her hair. "I used to brush my mother's hair," he said. "Do you like it brushed up from the neck, too?"

"No, we'll wait for my hanging for that. Tell me the rest of it."

Brushing, Henry told her what he knew, that the tale had originally been privileged information, but that later Catalina had spooked and decided she'd better tell the sheriff about it. But she was afraid to report it to the sheriff, so she asked Vargas to tell him for her.

Henry suddenly realized that she was quietly weeping. He put his arms around her and held her closely, murmuring.

"I'm cursed, Henry!" she wept. "She was the only witness I had. And she's turned against me! What am I going to do?"

"Well, so far, Vargas is waiting for me to tell him what to do. I think you should go over and tell him your story — and then stay on that side of the line. Let me talk to a lawyer on this side, and, er, explain what we've found to Bannock. Because everything we've found says that the Hunter killed Rip, with one single, unbelievable shot."

Frances turned, tears on her face, but laughing. "Oh, Henry! Couldn't you have come up with a better word than unbelievable He's got to believe it!"

Chapter Twenty

With all the determination and force of an intelligent woman, Frances declared that she would never return to Nogales. "I have shaken off the dust of that town forever!" she said.

They had reached the ranch yard in late afternoon. Henry was wearily unsaddling his Army mount, and Alejandro had carried Frances's saddle into the adobe-walled barn.

"By now, I am wanted for murder, on the word of a prostitute. My father is a subject for jokes, women snicker at me, and I expect I shall soon lose this ranch in bankruptcy court."

Even in her worn-out state she was beautiful, perhaps more so than before, since the deep shadows in her eyes and the thinness of her cheeks emphasized her fragility.

Henry said: "Don't be too sure about losing the ranch. Manion told me old Hum Parrish took some legal step to protect it. It's there in the papers. I'll look them over again."

"Hum Parrish is dead. A couple of thousand dollars of bad debts ago. The ranch is a corporation, true. But I don't know whether the trick will work."

"You're tired, Panchita. Tomorrow —"

"I've been tired for months. You're tired, too. Leave this town, Henry. Get on the train and go back to Kansas City. I told you there's a curse on the Wingards. No good will come of trying to help me."

Henry kissed her sunburned lips with his own dry, cracked lips. "Woman," he said, "where you go I go. If it has to be Costa Rica."

"No, Henry. I'm the bad luck lady. We have a little house in Hermosillo. I'll stay there and get a midwife's license."

"And how are you going to get to Sonora without going to Nogales?"

"There's a siding a mile from here where the train can be flagged. I'll catch it there tomorrow and just keep going. So that's settled!" she exclaimed. "Come inside now, and rest a while before you go on. And let your poor horse have a bait and a roll, too."

Henry ate and then slept for two hours. By the time he was stirring, the Mexican boy had saddled and groomed his horse, after washing its back and tending its hooves, and the big red dun was ready to travel. Henry stole to the door of Frances's bedroom and considered tapping on it — but Josefina appeared and shushed him.

"She sleeps, Señor Logahn. *Esta muy cansada! Vaya con Dios!*"

Before he went with God, however, Henry collected all the old ranch papers, and the silver pesos, and stuffed his saddlebags with them.

He rode into Nogales as a church bell was bonging out the hour of nine, ringing through the darkness as softly as though the bell were lined with velvet. In the warm and fragrant air, charcoal smoke and food smells created in him a mood of nostalgia for a place he had never lived. He could hear tired children fussing behind the lamplit windows of the little adobe houses. He stopped to have a cup of coffee with Alice Gary, whose hair was done up in curlers. They sat in the kitchen and talked softly in order not to disturb Miss Leisure and Arthur Cleveland. And as far as that went, he scarcely had the power to speak loudly, anyway. Allie, winding her alarm clock, saw it and said, "You look worn-out, Henry."

"I'm fine. Tell you whose health I am worried about, though. Milo Stockard's."

Allie hooted. "Don't worry about that old devil! Hasn't spent a sick day since he was a baby."

"He must have a doctor, though."

"Why?"

"Because some sawbones must have taken care of him when he blinded his eye."

"Oh, that. I think he went to Marcus Spanier. And of course the old idiot raised the dickens with Marcus when he couldn't save his eye."

Henry turned the alarm clock and read it. It was eight-thirty. "S'pose he'd still be up?"

"Stockard?"

"No, the doctor."

"Probably. When be's all through with his patients, be plays the French horn. They say that when he's driving out in the country on a call, you can hear him tooting for miles! The coyotes sing along with him! Really!"

"I believe it," Henry said. "My own father played the piccolo. He joined the Army to be a bandmaster. . . . Well, thanks for the coffee, Allie! Where is Dr. Spanier's office?"

"On Alamos." Allie told him how to find the house.

Henry rode until he found the peak-roofed house on the high side of Alamos Street. A stone retaining wall kept it from sliding down the hill. Behind the house he heard a windmill creaking. There were fruit trees in the front yard and a rose garden. A stained-glass fanlight glowed above the door. Though he heard no French horn tooting, be tied the horse to a cement hitching post and hiked up the steps to twist the handle of a brass doorbell.

A middle-aged woman appeared. When she heard Henry's name, she smiled. "Oh, you're the man who —"

"Probably." Henry smiled. He laid his hand about where his liver should be. "I've had malaria, ma'am, and lately I've noticed —"

"Come right in, Henry! The doctor's somewhere. He'll be so glad to meet you! He met your father at the fort once!"

Waiting in the hall, Henry sat on an elegant bottle-green love seat that lovers who could have mated on a rock might have found comfortable. In a moment a door opened and a dark-haired, middle-aged man looked out.

"Henry Logan!" he said. "What a pleasure! Captain Logan's son, I believe?"

Henry rose and offered his hand. "*A su servicio!* That about right?"

Dr. Spanier laughed. "*Mucho gusto!* And come right in."

In his surgery there was a long, low bench, glass-and-wood cases, bright steel tools laid out on white cloth, and racks of medicine bottles. Spanier placed a chair for him, and Henry sank onto it with a sigh.

"You should get more rest, Henry," the doctor warned. "Of course, championing young women can be tiring, I know. And you've had a tropical fever, I hear."

Henry was moving closer to having to finagle some information out of the doctor, and he hadn't yet worked out how to make his ten of diamonds look like an ace of spades. So he rubbed his liver again and said, "Yes, sir. You see, the Army doctors —"

Spanier raised his hands. "Don't tell me, Henry! I'll make my own diagnosis. Now, I can guess the state of your liver, but before I pass sentence I'm going to allow you one drink of your father's own brand of Irish whiskey."

He put a thermometer under Henry's tongue and then left the room. He returned with glasses, ice, and a bottle of Bushmill's and read the thermometer.

"Fine," he said. He poured the whiskey and raised his glass. "To your father!"

After the toast, the doctor began recalling the legend of Captain Black Jack Logan — his rich Irish tenor voice, his yarns, his Black Irish handsomeness. Yet he recalled, too, a strain of sadness in him, a loneliness and dissatisfaction.

"Of course, he should have been a full colonel," he said. "But somehow he was always passed over. And do you know the strangest thing of all?"

Henry shook his head. He knew something a lot stranger about his father than the doctor was likely to, but he let him tell his story.

"There was simply no way he could be induced to play the piccolo! But I heard him play, once — he played just for me, because I was an amateur musician, too. Henry, the sound was like poured silver — no, it was like the purest notes sung by the most talented mockingbird in creation, trilling to attract a mate!"

Henry's eyes filled, and he drank quickly. *Don't do this to me, Doctor!* Fatigue and worry had just about done him in. He wiped his lips, lowered the glass, and said, "I know why he wouldn't play. The goddamn Army tricked him. He joined to be a bandleader and musician, not to murder Indians. I think it was a protest. He wouldn't play a note, not even for the general's parties."

Dr. Spanier sighed. "I know, and it's really too bad. I may not be much of a horn player, but I'd miss it if I couldn't play it. . . . Well, Henry, about your physical problem. Let that be your last drink for a while. And take it easy, for heaven's sake — get more rest."

"I'll try."

"At least" — Dr. Spanier chuckled — "I hear there's no faulting your eye. Heard tell you shot the bejesus out of that pipsqueak Ambrose's golden ball! Couldn't you have made it his, er, balls?"

Henry laughed.

Then the doctor said something that led right into Henry's area of interest. He said, "Let's see what a good eye looks like. Sit tight."

He donned an ophthalmologist's mirror, adjusted a lamp, peered into Henry's eye, and murmured, "Beautiful! No floaters, absolutely clear vitreous humor! Macula like a diamond."

As he shifted the light to Henry's left eye, Henry said, "I hear General Stockard's got quite an eye, too. . . ."

"Yes. Rotten disposition, but a good eye. Well — he did have. You know about his loading accident?"

"Yes. Scorched himself pretty well, did he?"

Spanier laid down his instruments. He seemed to debate something. "Well, the flesh near his eye," he said.

"I don't understand."

"The eye itself is sound."

Henry felt a thrill so great that he had to seize the whiskey bottle and pour himself another inch of amber joy.

"But why the eye patch, then? Why did he

quit shooting? Surely he's not faking blindness?"

Spanier raised a cautionary finger. "Now, now, Henry! I didn't say that. I meant that the damage is in his mind — that fear of blindness turned off the lights in that eye! But he might as well have ripped out the cornea. He doesn't need the eye patch any more than the bust of Beethoven on my wife's piano needs spectacles."

"Then why does he wear it?"

Spanier winked at him. "Bid for sympathy. He'd kill you if you said it, but I think it's true. He's too tough to mourn his tragedy, but his ego was punctured. He's saying to men, 'If I don't challenge you anymore, you know why.' Now and then he comes in to ask what I've read in the journals. What can I tell him? The eye is undamaged! It wasn't even singed in the explosion."

In his room, Henry pored over every scrap of paper Lawyer Manion had given him, every onionskin and memo he had read while he was sick the previous week. What finally struck him was that the ranch was officially the Spider Cattle Corporation. Spider, Inc., this; Spider, Inc., that; John Manion, for Spider Cattle Corp.

At one point Frances Wingard Parrish became vice president of the corporation, even. And, of course, a quire of please-remits.

Most surprising, though, a written offer for the ranch, made by Milo Stockard, AUS, Ret., and Aaron Beckwith, Bank of Nogales. Apparently Ambrose wasn't even in it with the general — they were partners only in the newspaper.

Then, exhausted, he turned off the light and lay in the dark, mulling over what the doctor had told him. It was clear now that Stockard, as well as anyone else, could be the Hunter — that his eye was as perfect and as dangerous as ever! Tomorrow he would visit the *Globe* office and see whether that tarnished bottle-nose shell from the sniper's roost would fit the general's target rifle.

Deep in the night a vision of his father appeared before him.

Clad in a white planter's suit and sporting a fine wide-brimmed Panama hat, Captain Logan was standing in the *zaguán* of a big Spanish-style house. There was lawn, huge-leaved plants, gorgeous purple-flowered vines crawling over the house, and little black-haired servants, also in white, standing by, awaiting his orders. He heard wind chimes and birds singing. It was lovely! Was he dead? he wondered. Then his dad raised a revolver

— no, it was a silver piccolo! — pointed it at Henry, and made the popping sound with his lips that as a child Henry used to laugh over.

He blew a tune Henry loved, "Oh, Danny Boy," lowered the piccolo, and said, "Never give up, Henry. Get the payroll through."

"I'll get it through, Dad!" he promised. "Play it again!"

His father said, "It's really called 'Londonderry Air,' a nice Irish song, but her we go" — and with the notes of that lovely, heartbreaking tune in his head, Henry slept like a dead man, dreaming of cascades of silver pesos.

Chapter Twenty-One

On International Street, Henry saw Father Vargas pulling a wagon made of cast-off parts up the rutted street. The stores were open, though it was not yet nine o'clock, and the wagon was heaped with boxes and sacks of purchases. Bent forward, the priest strode along in his black cassock, holding a book close to his face. Henry stood among three others on a corner, waiting for the bank to open.

"Good morning, Father!" he called.

The priest looked up, smiled, and came to the sidewalk. In the cool sunlight they shook hands. Then Henry drew him aside, out of the hearing of the others. He was carrying an old briefcase of John Manion's, and Richard Parrish's bag of silver pesos.

"I have some news," he said. "I've been out to Spanish Church. I've done the metes and bounds, I've doped the wind and reckoned the trajectory of the bullet that killed Richard Parrish. And it would be impossible for Frances to have shot him with a revolver. The woman just thought she saw it happen."

"Yet she swears she did!"

"Impossible." Henry pointed. "The shot was made from a cliff *five hundred yards away!* I have the spent shell, and I think I know where the body is buried. I'm going to talk to Sheriff Bannock this morning, but if this woman broadcasts her lies, it may mean Frances Parrish will be jailed and have to hire a lawyer to get out. I thought," he said, "it might be possible for you to convince Catalina that she's wrong."

Vargas sighed. "Unfortunately, she was married a few days ago, Meester Logan! Her husband wants to sell the story to the newspaper. I fear he's already made arrangements."

Henry heard a lock rasp behind him, saw blinds being raised in the bank, and said, "This would be Ben Ambrose?"

"Yes. What in the world are you carrying, Meester Logan?" Henry chuckled. "Oh, just some money I'm about to deposit. Who's the lucky groom?"

"A man named Budge Gorman."

Henry had to wait a few minutes to talk to Aaron Beckwith. The bank lobby was paneled in dark wood, with a floor of black-and-white linoleum you could play chess on. At each brass-grilled wicket was a small china cuspidor. Tellers with paper sleeve-protectors were filling canvas bags with coins for merchants, but Beckwith was out of sight behind green drapes.

Henry stared out a window. Gorman! My God! Bouncing off his dream of marrying Frances, into the arms of a whore, just to tell her, "I don't want you anymore!" And then to complete his triumph by *selling* her downfall to the newspaper.

A gaunt man with a weathered face came to a gate in a walnut fence, pointed a finger at Henry, and went back into his green cubicle. He was seated behind a desk when Henry entered. Beckwith waved at a chair. Henry guessed from his cold eye that he knew him.

"What can I do for you?" Beckwith asked. He was no overweight, red-faced man of affairs whose appetites were in his face. He looked horn-hard, his features stained by wind and sun, and his eyes lead-gray in a poker face. The sleeves of his black coat were too short. He would look more at ease in a dirty canvas jacket and work pants, with a smoking branding iron in his hands. Yet his eyes avoided Henry's.

"It's about Mrs. Parrish's account . . ."
Henry began.

But Beckwith said, "Mrs. Parrish doesn't have an account with us."

"I think Spider Cattle company does, and she's the vice president. Am I right?"

"By Arizona law, it's her husband's account. Pretty close to defunct, anyway."

Henry placed the bag of pesos on the desk and patted it. "You'll find two hundred and fifty pesos in all here, to bring the balance up a little. Mrs. Parrish came across the money the other day."

"I'll have it counted and credited to Spider's account."

"Aren't you interested in where she found the money?"

"Not particularly."

"The sack was under her husband's bed!"

"Well — a temporary safe place, evidently."

"But where did it come from?"

Beckwith raised and dropped his hands. "Mr. Logan — it looks like a busy day. Was there anything else?"

"One or two things. I'm trying to help Mrs. Parrish get her finances squared away, and one of the things I noticed was an offer on the ranch signed by you and General Stockard. It's dated about five months ago."

Beckwith rolled a pencil between his palms.

"That's right. And a fair one, when you consider that we'd be assuming all the ranch's debts." Beckwith could be holding two deuces or four aces. His brown, stringy face revealed nothing.

"Why would you do that?" Henry asked, surprised.

"Because, goddamn it, they'll have to be paid before title to the ranch is clear!"

"But the ranch is a corporation — Spider Cattle Corporation. And all the bills I've seen were signed by Parrish himself — as an individual. The ranch doesn't owe anything, as far as I know."

Beckwith's face flushed. Henry had rocked him. He wasn't sure of his own ground, but he had startled him. "Where did you hear that?" the banker asked scoffingly.

"Hum Parrish's attorney told me the old rooster was such a gambler, he set up the corporation to protect the ranch against his poker losses."

"Well, I'd suggest you consult a Territorial attorney, Mr. Logan." Beckwith placed his hands flat on the desk.

Henry got up. But then he dug into the leather bag and drew out a handful of silver coins. "Did he deposit many of those government assay office drafts?" he asked.

"He didn't deposit any of them! He cashed

them. About all he ever deposited were the trust checks he received from Kansas City every month."

"Cashed the government drafts for gold?"

"No, dammit! We seldom see gold here. He cashed them for silver coins — pesos. Mr. Logan — adios, as we say on the border."

"Do you have the saying, on the border, 'salting'?" Henry asked. "As in salting a mine, to make it look richer than it is?"

"I'm not sure what you're getting at, but I do know that old mine is played out. When Stockard and I made our offer on Spider, we were interested in land. Because that's all there is out there."

"No, but if you look at those assay slips, I think you'll see the proportions of silver and copper in the bars he sold just about match that in sterling silver! In church artifacts, for instance."

"Pretty close, I suppose."

"Or Mexican coins. The numbers on these pesos tell how many parts of silver are in them — usually around seven- twenty in a thousand — sterling, that is. Same as what the assayer found in the ingots Rip Parrish was bringing him. Still, it's no secret that he gave a silver candlestick to Father Vargas, so maybe be was digging up treasure, not coins."

"I'm not a treasure hunter, Logan."

"Good thing you aren't. Because what Rip Parrish was doing was melting pesos, shaping them into ingots, and selling them to the government assayer. Then cashing the government drafts for more pesos to melt!"

Beckwith dug out a handful of pesos and looked at them. "I don't — that makes no sense at all. Why on earth —"

"To create a false impression!" Henry said. "Like salting a mine. Rip wanted people to think he had tons of silver out there. That he might not be much of a cattleman, but he sure knew where the silver was! In another few months he'd probably have been ready to put the ranch up for sale. What a shame some deadeye dick shot him before he could work his scheme."

Chapter Twenty-Two

Henry walked south from the bank to the *Globe* office and tried the door. He rattled it, then banged on it, peering through the mullioned glass panes. The place was dark. He turned to stare at the Frontera Hotel, rolling his shoulders. A man on the veranda was watching him. Henry gave a grunt of satisfaction and started for the hotel.

At a small round table of Mexican palm fiber and rawhide sat Ben Ambrose, a gray fedora on the side of his head. He was sipping coffee and nibbling a rolled tortilla and appeared to be reading a book. Yet his bearing was somehow not that of a successful editor taking his ease in the warm morning, but of a lonely and beleaguered man. He damned well should be lonely! Henry thought bitterly. Most people in the town feared him — did anyone love him? Was he married, and did his wife hector him, as others were afraid to? And it appeared that General Stockard had dropped him as a partner.

Which, however, might be the very thing that saved him from hanging.

Henry climbed the steps to the wide porch as Ambrose, in the shade of the wooden awning, watched him come. He placed his hand on the back of a chair and growled an invitation.

"Waiter'll be here in a minute," he said.

He bit down on the rolled tortilla, his lips flaring back from long-stained teeth as yellow as those of an old dog. His gray box coat hung open, and Henry glimpsed the butt of a small pistol in a slash in the lining. Looked like a British Bulldog, butt like a small banana, probably a .28-caliber. The jauntily waxed tips of his mustache did not match the emaciation of his face, the dried skin dark as jerked venison.

"How's the state of your health?" Ambrose muttered.

"Despite all," Henry said, "I'm feeling fine." He tried to see what the editor was reading, and sat back smiling. "Isn't that Latin? With your nature you can't be studying for the priesthood, so it must he the law."

The gaunt head came up. "It's neither."

"What is it, then? Homer?"

"Homer was Greek. It's about war."

"Don't you ever get enough? You should have tried Cuba, like Stephen Crane. He got a good book out of it."

"Crane's best book was about the Civil War, which he never saw. You don't have to leave town to find stories, Logan. Every man's life has a book in it, but most lives are dismal failures — every day a bungled patrol, every year a disastrous retreat. Why? Lack of basic military comprehension! Men fail because they think life is a friend, not an enemy."

"So my father learned. Why don't you write his biography? I hear tell he had a very exciting life, once he left the military."

"You're forgetting, I did your father in my book — a chapter, at least. He was a perfect example of the average man — no offense, Logan — in his case, of a capable military man who didn't understand that life is to be fought, not tootled away on a tin whistle. He let the brass push him around, pass him over for promotions, give him a dangerous job like paymaster in Indian country. Life is nothing but a goddamned enemy."

"How can I protect myself?" Henry grinned at Ambrose's rising excitement.

"Develop a battle plan! Set up a final firing line — the critical point beyond which you will not be pushed! Where you howl like a savage and take your dagger in your teeth.

What if you lose? Is it any worse than breaking your neck yawning?"

"Right!" said Henry. "Although . . . well, I'd have thought your golden globe was a final firing line."

Ambrose bared his stained teeth again in a grin like a monkey's. "Not at all. It was just a skirmish. Of no strategic importance whatever."

A waiter brought coffee and tortillas.

"Still," Henry said, "it's quite a comedown, isn't it? From riding with Stockard with your dagger in your teeth, to running a small-town newspaper with a Mexican cigarette in them. I used to see your articles in *Harper's Weekly,* and I read your book, but here you are — look at yourself, man — publishing recipes, biggest-turnip-in-Arizona stories, and vignettes of history! Was that your battle plan?"

The editor flipped his cigarette into the street and somehow made his shrug seem insulting. "I've done all right."

"Well, I've got a suggestion," Henry said. "Take your dagger in your teeth again and start setting type. I've got a story for you. You might call it 'The Killing of Rip Parrish.'"

He pulled a spent shell from his pocket and stood it upright on its base. "What do you think? That shell case is unique."

Ambrose turned it in his fingers, lips pursed. A bottlenose brass cartridge with a case as thick as his thumb, it looked like any other express shell, over three inches long, necked to take a paper patch or two. But he unwittingly touched what was strange about it when he ribbed the brass tube where the big shell throated down to the more common .45-caliber.

"Want my guess? A Sharps buffalo load."

"It used to be. But look at it closely. It's been redesigned for smaller but more dangerous game. The bullet from this shell killed Richard Parrish."

Ambrose tidied the corners of his mouth with thumb and forefinger, then wound the three hairs that comprised the tip of his right mustache. He recited, his voice mocking, "'I shot an arrow in the air, it came to earth I know not where.' How can a gunsmith possibly believe that the lead from this case came to earth in Rip Parrish's unworthy carcass? Did you find the body? Is he dead? I guarantee this would make a story, if you can back it up."

"I know where he's buried. I don't know how the general dragged him up there by himself, but who knows, maybe he had a cohort —"

He broke off as a thunderous explosion rolled and echoed along the street.

He had dodged enough artillery to recognize that it was a round from a fieldpiece. He yelled, *"Take cover!"* his heart bouncing up in his chest, and found himself on his knees, trying to crawl under the table. *He was back in the crotch of a tree, safety-belted, and a Spanish gunner was laying ranging shots on him.* Echoes rolled like distant thunder, coffee sloshed, and behind them windows rattled. On a brown Mexican hillside a mile away, a shell burst threw up a cloud of dirt.

"That old loony!" Ambrose groaned. "It's all right, Logan, we aren't being shelled. Stockard is going mad as a hatter. I wonder if he decided to put his senile wife out of her misery. Today's headline: THE HEADLESS HOUSEWIFE!"

Henry sat down again, his pulse still bounding. "Was that a shot from his famous target rifle?"

Ambrose coolly blotted his saucer with a napkin. "Not quite. He has this Civil War cannon, you see — mint condition. It squats on his lawn like a bulldog, and on New Year's Eve and certain important occasions he fires a round."

"What's he celebrating this time?" Henry

poured coffee from his saucer in to his cup.

"God knows. But I claim this calls for a beer."

Henry wiped his brow with his napkin. "I'll drink to that. My last alcoholic beverage, sir — there's a story for you!"

Ambrose shouted for the Mexican waiter, sent the coffee away, and ordered *cervezas de Anchor*.

Henry sipped the cold red beer with voluptuous enjoyment as Ambrose took out his silver hunting-case watch, read it, grimaced, and said, "Get on with your fairy tale, Sergeant. A man's coming to see me. If I understand it, you're *pretty sure* Rip Parrish has gone to his reward, you're *positive* you have the cartridge that killed him, and you'd *probably swear* that my ex-partner fired it."

"I'll draw you a picture," Henry said.

Ambrose found a fold of newsprint in his coat, and Henry adjusted his mechanical pencil. He smoothed the paper and reflected; then, with meticulous strokes; sketched the juniper stump that had become an executioner's chair. He drew a towering butte across the page from it and indicated with military symbols where a couple of trees interfered with a straight shot from the dome to the stump.

"All right," he said, "from the stump to the

top of the butte is over five hundred yards. Rip was sitting on the stump. It was dark. So to put the cross hairs on him, the general — let's call him the Hunter — would have had to aim on the campfire itself and allow about a foot and a half of elevation to reach his wishbone. He's using a Malcom 3X scope, probably — impossible to see it with iron sights."

He frowned. Sipped some beer. Then tapped the paper. "But look here, Ambrose! The trees are in the way."

"Aha!" Ambrose exclaimed. "'With a sneer the Hunter took from his saddlebag a magic target rifle that would fire around corners!'"

"Oh, no — the Hunter's used to solving tactical problems. He accepted the givens and broke the equation. It took time and money, but he was gambling for a ranch and what he thought was buried treasure. He started with a Sharps cartridge like this — old buffalo load, .50-caliber, a hundred and forty grains of powder, seven-hundred-grain lead slug. The kind of shell that kills at one end and cripples at the other.

"But he knew that to clear the trees, a cannonball like that would have to cut so high a trajectory that it would come into camp falling like a rock — damned near vertically, and without enough velocity for a sure kill. He needed a special load — the bullet had to be lighter, a little smaller, and propelled by a bigger charge of powder. Best to use a paper-patch shell, for maximum accuracy. With a load like that, the bullet would come in with about the force of a Colt .45 slug at close range. So that's what the Hunter invented. And the gun he showed me the other day would handle this — and no other shell you'll find. Because it's tailor-made."

Ambrose tossed the brass case on his palm. "You're wrong. This thing would never go into Milo's gun. The gun you saw is plain old '85 Winchester — common, ordinary .45-caliber. This is too fat. Try again. Of course, he could have used a different gun."

Henry felt a flush of armorer's fever. "Never! Shooters like him are married to their favorite guns. Have you ever really examined it? It's a .50-caliber now. Ever heard of the Browning brothers, of Ogden, Utah?"

Ambrose leered. "No! What bank did those rascals rob this time?"

"They're gun makers — the elite in the field. He had that old '85 rechambered by them. I almost saluted when I saw their little *BB* engraved on the wall of the rifle. They made it into a .50-caliber target rifle, necked down to .45 for the lighter load he had to have. Also, it's a paper-patch gun now — they throated it to make sure the patch contacted the rifling, to give it the spin he wanted for maximum accuracy." Blank-faced, Ambrose looked at him. "I'll be damned. I'll . . . I'll have to look at it. But surely you're not going to the sheriff with no more evidence than this?"

"Oh, there's more! *This* is the lead slug that went through Rip's brisket and buried itself in the chair. I dug it out yesterday, before a witness. Look at that thing!"

He dropped a deformed bullet on the table. In the dull gray flattened slug, small pockets of bone were embedded like chalk in a chunk of rock. Ambrose used his pencil to turn it.

"My God!" he said.

"You'll notice Frances Parrish's little F on the base."

Again Ambrose looked at his watch. "What about the possibility," he said, "that she shot Rip herself? This man I'm waiting for — he has a story about Parrish, too."

"Yes, Father Vargas told me about Catalina's hair-raising experience. Is Budge selling you her story? Then keep in mind that she was scared senseless and it was dark, so that she had no idea what was going on.

"Think about this, too: When Rip's body is exhumed, the path the bullet took through his carcass will prove either that Frances was hanging by one hand from the branch of a tree when she shot her husband, or that somebody else shot him from the bluff. The bullet was traveling downward — descending from a six — or seven-foot trajectory."

A couple of Mexican cowboys rode by. Ambrose lighted another cigarillo. "I'll tell you what I know for sure, Logan. But anything about the murder would be pure speculation on my part."

"That's all I'm asking."

"All right, this is the truth, naked as a jaybird: I do not know whether Parrish is dead or not! I do not know where he's buried, if indeed he's dead. If he is, I do not know who buried him. I agreed to go out with the Hunter, as you call him, but I warned him never to tell me about any game he shot. I wished he hadn't confided in me at all, but he did so because, without a spotter, he could have spent the rest of his life zeroing in for that shot. It's a half-hour climb to his roost. He made a dozen shots, and I waved a flag to tell him where he was hitting. Rip was at Spider, on one of his rare visits home — on conjugal business, I presume.

"When the Hunter had logged five shots in a six-inch circle, he started down — and I left. I came home. I suppose he stayed out there. Did he shoot him? I don't know. Is he blind in that eye? I don't even know that."

Henry sipped, wiped foam from his lip. "Tough old rooster. And an unbelievable shot. A single leaf could have spoiled it."

"And yet do you know what I wondered? Why Rip didn't notice the practice holes in the damned stump?"

"Because the Hunter filled each hole with a juniper twig and smoothed it off so flush, you couldn't see it without a magnifying glass. What do you think? Is that a story you can use?"

Ambrose looked down, his eyes closed as if in prayer. "Henry," he murmured, "I'd almost die to run that story. But not quite."

A man crossed the street and made for the hotel, walking slowly and giving Henry the impression that he was drunk but trying to walk sober. Ambrose's mouth twisted into one of his derisive grins and he touched the brim of his hat.

"Sheriff?" he called. "Friend of mine wants to pay his respects."

The man, on the steps now, made a choking sound, barely audible, a sort of anguished croak, and came toward the table, a very large man in black pants and a pinto horsehide vest ornamented with a star. He carried thirty pounds too much weight, most of it bulging above his silver and turquoise belt buckle. His red face was given an authoritative look by a thick gray mustache. He was puffing a bit when he reached the table and looked down at Henry, who remembered uneasily what Frances had told him about her father having removed a growth from the sheriff's throat. He appeared to be a sick man, uncomfortable with his goitrous belly — embarrassed, no doubt, about his voice.

"You've read about the famous Henry Logan, Sheriff," said Ambrose. "Actually, I'm afraid he's not as bad as I cracked him up to be. In fact, Henry's rather astute"

Sheriff Bannock forced grotesque sounds from his throat. "Hello, Henry," he said, croaking. "Stick around. Town needs 'stutes."

"Reminds me of a joke of Rip Parrish's," said Ambrose." 'Be alert,' he would say. 'The country needs 'lerts.'"

Bannock whispered, "Too damn many 'lerts as it is! Think I hear one. Coming, in fact."

Up the street, a man was shouting. On the walks, men laughed. A familiar overalled figure in a black Civil War hat came tramping up the middle of the street, waving a paper and bawling, "Catalina! When I find you, you bitch, I'll whip your ass!"

"Disgusting," said the sheriff, and when the editor suggested that he join them, he shook his head and whispered, "meeting someone."

"Christ," Ambrose said through his teeth. "Now I've got to tell that hound-faced idiot I won't buy his story."

"Why not, if you're not using mine?"

"Because I know his is nonsense!" Ambrose clutched Henry's forearm. "I wish to God I could run it, but . . . well, for one thing, I don't think Milo's quite sane anymore. That cannon of his — think I want a cannonball right through my shop, and me in it?"

"I'll sleep on your roof till he's locked up."

"He won't be locked up — never. He'd be in Mexico before I ran the second installment. But first he'd kill me. If I dared, though, I'd run an installment every day for a week! Maybe as fiction, at first! *Two Days in the Life of a Hunter.*'"

Ambrose gazed into the sky, pain and glory in his eyes. "He prepares meticulously — then, on the last day . . ." In his hands he held an imaginary target rifle. "'*The Hunter lowered his smoking gun and watched as his target toppled slowly from the stump, his hand still plucking at the strings of his banjo. . . .*'" And that's when I'd tell who the characters were. But you see, Henry — the risk is just too . . . too . . ."

Henry said, "I've got a better story still. Take your dagger in your teeth, Ben, and run it first. Do you like stories about men

254

disappearing into Mexico?"

"What's this?" Ambrose looked at the blemished envelope Henry had laid before him. In the upper right-hand corner was a blue-green stamp, heavily canceled and obviously foreign. He turned the envelope to scrutinize the reverse, where the word CENSORED had been stamped, along with some Army lieutenant's name.

He smirked. "Souvenir of the late war? Some girl who thought the world of you, but —"

"It was from my father — reached me in Cuba."

Ambrose shrugged. "Held up in some Arizona post office for years?"

"No, no, Ben — it came from Costa Rica, while I was in Cuba."

"Then I guess I don't know what you're talking about."

"I made a copy of this letter, and if you do a nice job on the general, I'll let you have this letter and the picture he sent with it. It's signed 'Your loving papa, Captain John "Black Jack" Logan.'"

"Your stepfather?"

"No, my real father. You see, Ben — *he wasn't in that barn when the outlaws burned it!* He was up in the rocks, hiding the payroll bag! Those murderers weren't

Indians, either — they were outlaws. Pulled the shoes off their horses' hoofs to lay it onto Indians. . . ."

Ambrose looked up at the hillsides above the pass; his eyes roved the fleecy morning clouds and came back to Henry's face, and he looked like someone else now. Some god he had fervently believed in had been revealed as a myth.

"Oh, my *God!*" he said.

But now Budge Gorman stood before the hotel, shirtless and black-hatted, waving a hairy arm at the editor. "We're all set, Ben!" he bawled. "I got her John Henry on it!"

Ambrose muttered, "In a pig's eye!"

Chapter Twenty-Three

Budge Gorman slapped the paper he carried on the table before Ben Ambrose, stepped back, and stared at both men with his head tipped up and his eyes rolling to show the whites.

"What have we here?" said the editor.

"Look 'er over, Ben!" shouted Gorman. "It's my wife's sworn statement!"

"I can hear you, Budge — have mercy on our eardrums Has she signed the statement?"

Gorman pulled up a chair, turned his head, and bawled, *"Mozo!* Where's that goddamn waiter?" He smelled of horses, manure, wine, and sweat. His long, mournful face was unshaven and his hair straggled from beneath the Grand Army hat.

"Patience," the editor said with a sigh. "He's coming. Let's see now. . . ."

"Right there! Are you blind? The X! Catalina can't write her name, either, so she makes an X, like me. Ain't that what you wanted?" He gave Ambrose an anxious look and added, "I always use an X myself, and then somebody writes, 'Alonzo Gorman, his mark.' I reckon you'll have to write her name down."

Shaking his head, the editor said quietly, "No, Budge, because I didn't witness it. And that isn't an X, man, it's a plus sign — like you use yourself. You made it, didn't you? Not Catalina." He chuckled, patting Gorman's arm amicably.

Gorman pounded the table with both fists. "No, you idiot! She done it herself. What's the matter with you?"

Henry saw clearly that the meeting could only end in disaster. He realized that the editor carried a pistol with good reason. As he sat back, looking more like a gambler than a journalist, he said quietly, "Settle down, Budge. The sheriff happens to be inside the hotel, if we should need him. You've got to understand that I cannot run a bald-faced accusation of murder without a signed statement by the person I'm quoting. Can you comprehend that?"

"But you promised me! Is it the fifteen dollars? Is that what's the matter?"

"As it stands, you couldn't pay me to publish the charge. In fact, I now believe you should report Catalina's story to Sheriff Bannock, and

I'll run the story when a warrant is issued for Frances Parrish."

Breathing hard, his lips pooching out with the exhalations, the stableman turned the paper and frowned at it. Then he threw his hat on the floor and shouted at Henry: "You poisoned my water hole, you bastard! Everything was all right till you turned him around!"

Henry said, "Ambrose is right, Gorman. It has to be signed before a witness, or he'll be in hot water."

"The woman did this! She got you to sour things for me. Fixing to get even with me for . . . for turning her down." Almost sobbing, he said, "God*damn*, I hate a woman like that! She'll tease you, and . . . and practically flop down on her back for you, and then scream like a bitch coyote that you molested her!"

"Hey," Henry said. He made a gesture with his thumb.

"You'd better leave, Budge," Ambrose said. "I'll explain it later, when you've cooled out a bit."

"The goddamn chippy has been slandering me! Admit it, Logan!"

"Budge," Ambrose snapped, "you're drunk. Take off."

"Slut!" Budge shouted. "Dirty, whoring slut! I'm sick of her running this town! "

Henry hit him openhanded with both palms,

and Budge fell back to the floor at the top of the stairs. He rolled onto his belly, like a beetle trying to right itself, and Henry saw the holstered gun he wore between his hip pockets. Budge got on to one knee and one foot, and Henry put Rip's nice alligator boot in his side and sent him sprawling down the steps. He followed as Gorman rolled onto the walk, bellowing like a mad bull, and placed his boot upon the man's Adam's apple, choking off his shouts. Gorman's left hand dug at his calf muscles, but his right hand was trying to pull the revolver.

Men were calling back and forth to each other, like boys on a play-ground. But those closer to the action were backing away.

"If you pull that gun, Gorman," Henry shouted, "I'll drive your Adam's apple through your spine!"

But Gorman kept tugging at the revolver, gagging, eyes bulging. What next? Henry wondered. If he pushed any harder, he would kill the man. If he didn't, Gorman might kill him.

Before he decided on a move, Gorman got the gun out. It was a five-inch-barrel Peacemaker that had lost most of its bluing. Henry drove his boot deeper into his throat as Gorman gagged, trying to cock the revolver. Through the uproar Henry heard a desperate,

260

croaking voice warning, "Cut that out, Gorman! Drop that."

Henry applied more pressure against the stableman's throat. Tears streamed from his eyes as Gorman tried with both hands to cock the gun. Henry heard it click like a beetle, and he dropped to his knees, getting out of line. He reached over to pound his fist into Gorman's nose, as the gun roared. Across the street, a window shattered. Men were vanishing from the sidewalk, and they faced each other on their knees, squared off like two fighting cocks in the pit. Gorman was having trouble seeing, because of the tears flooding his eyes. Blood poured from his nose.

A small-caliber gun made a spiteful crack. The Colt spun from Gorman's grasp. Henry snatched it up and hurled it into the street. Sheriff Bannock stepped in and rapped Gorman over the head with the barrel of his Colt. Gorman sat back on his heels, dazed, then sagged forward on to all fours.

Henry got to his feet, gasping. He looked up; Ben Ambrose stood on the hotel porch, a small, nickeled revolver in his hand — the British Bulldog he had seen in his coat. It was he, not the sheriff, who had shot the Colt out of Gorman's hand. Henry wondered whether he would have mixed in someone else's fight if a story had not been at stake.

They sat in the sheriff's office, where Henry had just signed his statement of the altercation. In the rear, behind a thin wall, Gorman was shouting in a cell.

"Listen to him," the sheriff croaked. "Hydrophobia skunk's got a cleaner mouth than that."

He was holding a cold beer someone had brought him in a large sweating schooner. He had shooed everyone out of the office and locked the door. The room was steeped in an aromatic tobacco smell, a miasma sacred to the memory of a thousand cheroots that had perished here. He was lighting one now, taking a rest from writing his report.

Gorman bawled, *"Rotten whore plugged her husband!"*

Bannock whispered, "Will you tell him for me that he's going to the asylum in Tucson if he can't control himself any better than this?"

The cawing voice reminded Henry of a crow that had picked up a little English. He walked to the rear door and shouted, "Sheriff says shut up or you'll go to the loony bin, Alonzo!"

Budge shouted back, *"He's got no jur'sdiction over me, anyhow! Marshal Osterman's gonna hear about this!"*

Bannock pressed his fingertips against his

eyeballs, as though they smarted or he was very tired. "He's right," he whispered. "But the marshal's out of town. I'll have to let him go in an hour or two. But he's let off steam now, and he'll settle down. Always that way."

Henry said, "I don't believe I myself can settle down, though, until he stops bad-mouthing Frances and accusing her of murder. That's slander."

Bannock whispered, "They're all saying that, the ninnies! I had no use for her father, but the woman is not better or worse than any other person of the female persuasion. Intelligent enough, I have no doubt, for a woman."

"My wife seen it! Dirty bitch shot him with his own Colt!"

Bannock made a tired gesture with one finger. "In the storeroom," he said, "you'll find a bucket with some soapy water in it. Would you just heave that over him?"

Henry went through the door in the rear. In a shadowed strap-iron kennel bolted to the floor of the storeroom, he could make out the hairy, roving, beastlike form of the stableman, looking like a particularly revolting sideshow freak in a cage. Gorman began swearing at him and rattling the flat iron bars. Henry looked around. In the shadows near the alley door he spotted a bucket with a brush floating in it. He set the brush on the floor, picked the bucket up by the bale, and gave Budge a steady look.

"What were you saying about Mrs. Parrish?" he asked.

"*Logan, you gonna be the saddest son of a bitch in Nogales if —*" Henry hurled the bucket of water. Gorman spluttered and choked.

Henry said, "Sorry, Alonzo," and went back to the sheriff, wagging his head. He saw Bannock replacing a small bottle of brown liquid in a drawer, wiping his lips and grimacing. He felt deeply sorry for him, with all his troubles, not the least of which was that he was dying of cancer of the throat. He supposed that Frances's infamous papa must have known it and done what he could, which was not much.

Henry watched the sheriff begin to write again.

"You know," he said, "I believe we can put a stop to this gossip, Sheriff. Wouldn't you like to clear the books on the Richard I. Parrish case? I gather it's causing you a world of trouble."

"I can clear the book. When I find him." Bannock sipped some more beer.

"I think I can help you there. I happen to know where the man's buried."

"No!"

"He's buried in the graveyard at Spanish Church. Frances Parrish told me about his apparent death, but I think she should be the one to give you the story."

"Are you a Pinkerton agent, Logan?"

"No. Still a gunsmith. But I've got the bullet that killed him, and the shell that fired it."

He placed the articles on the sheriff's desk, and Bannock examined them. "For God's sake!"

"I'll tell you how I found these when I have Mrs. Parrish here to attest to the story."

"Is it your plan. To dig up the entire. Cemetery out there?" asked the sheriff.

"No, sir. I have a specific grave in mind. His name is on it as plain as day."

"Parrish's?"

"Well, it says RIP, which of course stands for 'rest in peace.' But somebody who thinks he's pretty clever might think that was just the ticket. Somebody who trades on his daring — fires off cannons at will right in town. Get an order, Sheriff, and we'll go out there and dig. How about tomorrow morning?"

The sheriff groaned. "Nasty thought — dig up a ripe corpse and carry it home. Lord . . ."

"Get some rubberized canvas. We handled

265

plenty of aging bodies in Cuba — corpses ripe as Camembert."

In the back room, Gorman came to life again, but now he sounded like a changed man. "Sheriff? Can I talk to you?"

Bannock shook his head, and Henry called, "He says no, Budge."

"But it's very important. I'm sorry for the fuss I caused. I won't do it again."

"Go to sleep," Henry called. "Is he really married?" he asked Bannock.

"Are you asking, 'Who'd marry him?' A whore, that's who. He had some sort of falling-out." Cough. "Out with Frances Parrish. I reckon he thought she'd consider herself lucky. Marry a dashing moron horse handler like him. So a couple of days ago. He goes over to Bean Town and gets drunk and marries this poor soul. Where can I find you, Logan?"

He was gasping, his face pallid and moist. He wiped his brow on his sleeve. Henry had deep doubts about his ability to make the grueling ride to Spanish Church.

"I'm staying at Alice Gary's."

"Excellent cook. Very fine lady," Bannock whispered.

"For a woman?" Henry smiled.

Bannock smiled but looked puzzled. Was this outlander joshing him?

"But I'll be at the *Globe* for a while. Maybe

I can help Ambrose set type."

Henry smiled in reflection. "You know, Sheriff, I had a little printing set once, when we lived at Fort Bowie. I remember making up some stationery for my father for Christmas. 'John B. Logan, Captain, U.S. Army' it read. Had a letter from him on that very stationery a couple of years back. He'd saved it, all these years. I don't mind admitting I shed a tear or two."

He had reached the door and was unlatching it when the sheriff called, "Don't you mean . . . more like ten years ago?"

"No. Little better'n two. Read the *Globe* tomorrow," said Henry with a wink.

Chapter Twenty-Four

Frances and Josefina were packing the things Frances could not imagine living without. Late sunset tinted the windows. Both women broke down and wept from time to time, and Frances, packing books in an old trunk, had to stop and open each book and read a few lines her father had loved — mostly poetry she had been raised on.

> *I am part of all that I have met;*
> *Yet all experience is an arch where-*
> *through—*
> *She walks in beauty, like the night of*
> *cloudless climes and starry skies —*
> *My heart leaps when I behold a rainbow*
> *in the sky.*

And one of Dr. Wingard's favorites, from *Verses on the Death of Dr. Swift:*

He never thought an honour done him
Because a Duke was proud to own him;
Would rather slip aside, and choose
To talk with wits in dirty shoes!

Lovely! It almost described Henry. Would he come down to Hermosillo to visit her? To press his suit; as they said? She was sure he would, and she smiled as she imagined his appearing at her barred window some night. . . .

Two trunks were packed with books now, and her nice silver toilette set of brushes, combs, and mirror. No clothes yet — she had clothes in Hermosillo. She wrapped in tissue paper some little dancing shoes that had been her mother's, pink satin and ribbon. Souvenirs from *bailes* in Hermosillo.

Then she picked up her mandolin and held it to her breast, biting her lip; strummed it and found it out of key; looked for her pitch pipe but couldn't find it; and managed to tune it after a fashion.

Josefina murmured, *"Las Mananitas, Panchita!"*

Frances strummed a few twanging chords and sang the beginning of the beloved Mexican folk song. Then they wept again, in each other's arms. Alejandro tapped on the doorjamb, pointing toward the front of the house.

"Hay un soldado con dos caballos, y un canon!"

"Dónde?"

"Alla! En frente! Lo apunta a la casa!"

A soldier with horses pointing a cannon at the house? He must be joking. Could it be Henry? Hardly, though she was hoping he would appear with some money for her trip. He'd offered to exchange the bag of pesos for gold pieces, so much easier to carry when you traveled. Then for some reason she slung the mandolin over her shoulder, *estilo paisano*.

Wake up, Frances — the cannon! With all the distractions, her mind would not stay fixed on anything. She hurried into the parlor and pressed close to a window. Beyond a thicket of cactus and mesquite enclosing the house, a piece of machinery, red and black, gleamed in the dusk. She saw a pair of tall wheels and a cannon barrel, which seemed to point directly at her window. Alejandro was right: It *was* a cannon! A couple of draft horses stood at a distance, near a dusty caisson. A guidon, yellow and black, flapped indolently on a staff fixed to the caisson.

The cannoneer — if that was what he was — stood behind the piece, a rifle slung across his back, the lanyard in one raised hand, a revolver in the other. He wore a tan uniform, a curl-brimmed field hat — and an eye patch.

Instinctively, as his hand jerked at the lanyard of the cannon, she screamed and put her hands over her ears.

There was a flash — a sudden shocking roar — a cloud of smoke and dust rushing toward the house like a whirlwind. The windows rattled. Dust sifted from the roof beams. She heard something go whistling over the ranch house, and a moment later a smell of brimstone tainted the air.

General Stockard now began shouting. She uncovered her ears but could not distinguish the words. She went to Josefina, who was weeping in the middle of the room.

"It's all right!" she told her. "It's just that crazy old general. *Oiga — traigame la carabina de Señor Reep —*"

". . . authority of the power vested in me . . ." she made out, and saw Stockard pointing his revolver at the house.

Through the window she screeched, "Jost a meenute!" in the old accent of her childhood.

When she had the gun in her hands and was warily pulling at the loading lever, Josefina begged her not to go out, but she persisted.

"An officer will never harm a lady." (Except, of course, his wife: advice from her mother, a Southern lady who lived by a library of Tennessee myths.) But she was certain that, with his whole being steeped in militarism, General Stockard would at least not kill her. Whereas if she tried to hold the fort against his cannon . . .

She opened one of the massive double doors and stepped out to stand before it, carbine at port arms, mandolin slung across her back. She was struck by the drama of the scene: Behind the cannon stretched a sky steeped with the black-and-gray tones of a coming thunderstorm. The cannon, still leaking smoke, pointed into this threatening sky as if to challenge it.

The general strode forward and confronted her from a few yards away. "Attention!" he said.

With a sober face, Frances held the carbine vertically before her.

"*Si, mi general,* " she said, smiling to placate him.

"Speak English, woman!" roared the general. "By the powers vested in me, I declare this ranch spoils of war. I now ask you to lay your weapon on the ground and take two paces back."

He is insane! she thought, and hesitated. Dare she go unarmed in the presence of a lunatic? As she tried to decide, he settled the matter by firing his revolver in the air. Frances hastened to lay the gun in the dirt, took one pace back, and bumped into the door.

"Where is the boy I saw?" Stockard demanded.

"Alejandro? He's just a Mexican boy. Do you need him?"

"You don't have to be white to raise a flag, ma'am!"

Alejandro came out and helped hoist a large flag to the top of the pole.

It snapped loudly in the wind. Stockard saluted, and Frances swung the mandolin around, tried to raise her hand but could not, and finally got the instrument into present-arms position. Then, inspired, she began to softly play and sing the national anthem. Stockard seemed surprised but stood fast until she finished.

Then he said, "I declare you under arrest."

"Why, General?"

"You are charged with the murder of your husband. A Mexican woman swears to this."

"She is wrong," Frances said. "But for the time being, I want to ask you a favor. I was planning to leave on tomorrow's train, to move to Hermosillo. If you would permit me to do that, I would not bother you here, of course. I would be completely out of your way."

"I can't permit that. I don't want you in this town." Stockard paused to light a cigar. The brimstone smell of the match arrived almost as unnervingly as the cannon fumes.

"But you see," said Frances, "I often flag the train at the siding. They'll stop for me."

Stockard's fingernails at his beard. "Very well. How early do you need to leave to catch the train?"

"About seven."

"I warn you, though, madam — a state of war exists. If you or any of your servants attempts to trick me, you'll be shot. Go to your room and pack."

He lifted his yellow-and-black guidon from the socket in the caisson and carried it into the house behind her.

But in a half hour the general rapped on the door, and she opened it to see him standing a foot away with a revolver pointed at her. A whimper escaped her. "Can you cook?" he barked.

"Of course!"

"Well — throw something together for lunch."

Stockard closed all the shutters and drapes, so that when the food was ready, about two o'clock, lamps burned in the parlor and a carbide light hissed above the long harvest table in the dining room. The four of them sat in silence before platters of Mexican food and thin-sliced beefsteak cooked *carne asada* style.

The general cleared his throat and said grace, with references to fields of honor, enemies to be smitten, thews to be cloven, fortresses and tents of the wicked to be stormed, and, finally, quitting oneself as a man.

Then he reached up as though to scratch the back of his neck, and pulled a knife from a scabbard between his shoulder blades. He tapped the point on the table and said, "Amen."

He is absolutely insane, thought Frances.

As they ate, she kept hearing sounds, real or imaginary, outside. Yet she was not wishing Henry back — rather, she was hoping he would not storm the place and be murdered. In any event, she was leaving here, once and for all. She had never felt that she owned it, belonged to it. She belonged to medicine, and that was over, too, in this country.

She thought she understood, now, what was going on in the general's mind.

He was simply taking the ranch by force. His fieldpiece stood in the yard, his bumble-bee-hued pennant over the barrel. He would hold the ranch, anticipating her going to prison, and then dare anyone to bother him, while he set up some kind of deed to the place. And in a country where force and intimidation meant nearly everything, he might succeed.

But she managed to smile. "How is your wife, General?"

Stockard suddenly swiveled toward a window and went into an attitude of listening. Then he shrugged. "Emily? Loony," he said. "Losing her home is what unhinged her mind."

"Oh, I am sorry," Frances said. "Will you be bringing her back?"

"Of course. It's her home. I think you should know, dear lady, that I am not here on a show-the-flag mission. My partner will be filing suit against Spider Ranch in a few days for nonpayment of debts."

"That would be Mr. Ambrose?"

The general bared his teeth and made a slashing gesture with his knife. "Pah! That nincompoop. I lost all respect for him when he let that Kansas City gunsmith bluff him out. In the matter of the ranch, I've signed a partnership with Beckwith, the banker."

"How can you have a partnership on something you don't own?" Frances asked. "As soon as Richard is declared dead, I'll have enough money to pay off my debts. Then you won't have any hold at all on the ranch — real or . . . illusionary."

"Will you have three thousand dollars to pay off debts?"

Frances felt a tingle, enjoying seeing that

man storm into the trap Richard had set three years ago. "No, but I owe only a few hundred. Why three thousand?"

The grin that opened in the general's tough, short beard, a growth like overcropped curly gruma grass, looked more like a grimace of pain. "That's the approximate amount of the gambling debts of your late husband's that Beckwith has bought up."

"Gracious! Where?"

"From here to San Francisco. Rip's old haunts. Everywhere he went, he left gambling debts, IOUs, and then got out of town. Beckwith thought he could swing the matter by himself, but I convinced him he needed a partner. He put in the money. I agreed to do the groundwork."

Frances smirked. "I was worried for a moment. It's a shame about those debts, but they're no problem of the ranch corporation. Did you know Spider Ranch is a corporation? Rip's Uncle Hum set it up to protect himself against his own gambling losses — or any other *personal* debts, as opposed to those incurred by an officer of the corporation. I'm the vice president."

Stockard raised a piece of beef on the point of his knife, frowned at it a moment before shrugging. "Makes no damned difference. We'll make it work. It'll work. . . ."

"With cannons, maybe. Not in court." Then Frances gasped and raised her hands defensively. The general was on his feet, Colt in his hand. But he wasn't after her; he had heard something. He went to the window and crouched below it, raising his head just enough to peer out. Frances heard horses whickering.

Stockard strode back and turned off the hissing carbide ceiling lamp. The incandescent mantle began to expire slowly, cooling from white to yellow to red, and suddenly the room was dark. "Stay where you are!" he hissed.

He resumed his watch, until a man shouted out in the night, "General Stockard! It's me, Gorman!"

Now, Frances thought, *the roster of lunatics is complete. Now unless the general's code forbids letting women prisoners be molested, I may have to die fighting him off. And this time there is no escaping.*

She could smell the stableman before she saw him, standing with the general at a long table in the dim parlor. He brought with him a powerful odor of iodoform, which caused her to search until she found a dirty bandage around his right hand. She and Josefina had washed the dishes, and now she was heading back to her room when Gorman saw her and shouted, "There's the bitch who's responsible for the whole kit and boiling!"

Frances kept moving toward her bedroom door, but Gorman blocked her way. "You don't know when you're well off, do you? You've poisoned the whole town against me! And now you're after the general!"

"I have no idea what you mean. Let me pass, please."

"Don't you move!" Gorman strode to the table and picked up a long sheet of paper, evidently a proof of a headline for the newspaper. He came back with the proof stretched between his upraised arms, like a banner across a street, and thrust it close to her face. She could smell damp paper and printer's ink.

"This is what I mean!"

The headline type was enormous. Below it were some additional head lines in smaller type.

STOCKARD ACCUSED OF MURDERS

KILLING OF RIP PARRISH, 40 APACHES CHARGED!

Sheriff Issues Warrant!

Mystery Letter Starts Investigation!

The general took it quietly, almost as though

279

he failed to comprehend Gorman's excitement. He read the headline, wadded and discarded it, and said stiffly to Frances: "Kindly wait on the settee until I need you."

So she sat tensely on the black leather sofa, hearing Josefina rattling things in the kitchen, listening to Budge Gorman's threats and boasts.

"Next time I see that tinhorn gunman, General, I'll just take and tell him, 'Kiss my behind!' And if he don't do it, I'll lay him out cold this time!"

Stockard had looked at him and said, "What happened to your hand?"

It was wrapped in a dirty strip of linen — the source, apparently, of the powerful fragrance of iodoform in the room. Budge looked at it.

"Oh, uh — horse bit me," he muttered.

When he started on another threat, the general said, "Have you ever been in the army, Gorman?"

"For a while. . . . 'At's where I learned about horses — Fort Bowie, Fourth Cavalry." Nodding eagerly.

"Would you like to join the headquarters detachment I'm planning to commission?"

"Yes, sir! What, uh — when's this going to be?"

"Right now. Be quiet while I iron out some

problems. Why don't you sit down by the window and watch our flank?"

On the long table, the general unrolled a map he had brought from town. It was a topographical map and he studied it under a magnifying glass, from three different angles, before he straightened, raised his knife, and brought it down to stand quivering in the table at an intersection on the map.

"There!" he said.

Then he sat at the table and wrote, using a field desk such as Dr. Wingard had always traveled with. Considering the import of the news from town, he was remarkably cool, thought Frances. Was the story true?

The general asked: "Do you have any spirits in the place?"

"Yes. My husband kept a few bottles. What would you like?" She got up and went toward the kitchen.

"I'll find it. Stay where you are."

He came back with a bottle of whiskey and two glasses. Gorman chortled when he saw that they were going to have a drink. Stockard poured a couple of fingers in each glass, and they toasted the nation's commander in chief. Then he pulled his long-barreled Colt and said, "Let's see if liquor affects my shooting eye."

He snatched off the eye patch and threw it at Frances's feet. He took aim on an antelope's head on the wall to the left of the stone fireplace. Without appearing to aim, he drilled out its right eye. Frances screamed, and Budge covered his ears, then laughed.

"Bull's-eye!" he yelled.

Stockard smirked. "All right. That's settled. Henry Logan had better be as good as he says he is. Because he's going to meet me on the field of honor."

Frances rose from the settee. "Henry has nothing to do with all this, General! He was just trying to find Richard, and I don't believe he ever did."

"*He* thinks so, ma'am. Don't worry, he'll have an equal chance with me. We're both sharpshooters, and we understand field tactics."

Rip's carbine stood against the wall just inside the door, where the general had placed it after disarming Frances. He now checked it out, made sure it was fully loaded, and carried it to the table.

"What're you going to do?" asked Gorman, awed.

"The question is — what are *you* going to do for your commanding general?"

"Anything, sir!" Gorman leveled off his Grand Army hat and came to attention.

"First we'll swear you in."

The general took a hair bracelet of some kind from his left wrist. "Wear this wristlet from now on. It's woven of Apache hair, by my own wife. Though she thought it was horsehair." He chuckled. "Jesus, she'd have been shocked!"

Out of his depth, Budge rubbed at the bracelet on his hairy wrist and muttered, scratching. "Sumbitch itches."

"Of course it itches! That's the whole idea. I've worn it ever since I saw my first white man scalped by Indians. When I took my first Apache, I scalped him and brought the nasty thing home. The itching reminds you that they're still out there, Gorman — they haven't changed one damn bit! Wear it with pride!"

He folded a piece of paper, gave Budge a sketch he had made, and said, "Here are your orders, Sergeant Gorman."

Budge glanced at Frances. "Sir, I —"

"That's all right, I'll read it to you. The map explains all you really need to know. Can you read maps? Good. You are to go out to Spanish Church — immediately — and set up my command post where you see the X."

"Yes, sir. But what . . . what's a command post?"

"In this case, it's a carbine — the one you're holding. By the way, take it off safety when you get there. Leave it exactly where I've marked. . . ."

"But that's —"

"Are you questioning my orders?"

"I'm sorry, sir. Sure, I can read it. I draw maps all the time to show people how to get from here to there in town, and I can read 'em, too. The Army taught me."

"Good soldier, Gorman. Now, then. When you've accomplished your mission — I would guess that will be about seven this evening, just after dark — take the short route to town. Don't come back here — I won't be here. Find Sergeant Logan and give him this paper. He'll know what to do. Then go to the stable and wait."

Budge poured himself a bit more whiskey, but Stockard threw it into the cold fireplace. "You're on duty, Sergeant."

"Sir, what about the woman? She knows all the trails out here. Maybe she should go along and guide me. . . ."

Stockard chuckled. "Oh, you're a sly one, Sergeant. What I like about you. No, I'll need her myself. . . ."

Frances wondered whether she could reach the little nickeled derringer Henry had given her before the general satisfied his need for her. She was ready to turn her back on all her instincts and training and take his life, if it were the only way to save her own — and Henry's.

Gorman saluted and grabbed the carbine by the barrel, but the general said, "Not yet. Mrs. Parrish, do you have any paraffin in the house?"

"For . . . for putting up fruit only. That kind?"

"That kind. Stay put — I'll find it."

He carried the carbine into the kitchen. Soon, while Gorman sat eyeing her with his lunatic grin, she smelled the paraffin. Shortly afterward, he returned with the gun, turned it over to Budge, and dismissed him.

He told Frances, "Tell the Mexican boy to saddle your horse."

By the time Alejandro brought the horse to the door, Stockard had found a pair of manacles among the supplies in the ammunition wagon. "I hope you won't be too uncomfortable, ma'am," he said.

Chapter Twenty-Five

In the office of the *Arizona Globe*, Henry and the editor were fitting type into little trays Ambrose called "sticks." Henry puzzled out Ambrose's scrawled lines on newsprint and then looked for letters in the wooden hives in which they were sorted.

"Upside down and backward," Ambrose had instructed him. "You'll get the hang of it. Use the mirror if you have to."

"How long will this take?" It went so infernally slowly that Henry thought it might take a week to set the type for a mere column.

"All night," Ambrose said. "By seven o'clock I'd like to have the story in the window and at least a few dozen sheets printed."

Then he laughed, looked at the ceiling, and cried, "Oh, my God, it's going to be wonderful! Next week we'll finish up the Black Jack Logan story. And on to my book!"

Time passed, the last green light in the

sky faded, and Ambrose turned on yellow pulsing bulbs screwed into goosenecked stands. The sharp edges of the little pieces of type were beginning to make Henry's fingertips sore. He was eager to hear from someone how Stockard had taken the news that he would be charged with murder, for by now he must know it.

Sheriff "Whispering George" Bannock was getting a warrant from the judge, at his home.

Bailed out by his Grand Army friends, the stableman had come straight from the jail to the office and offered to accept ten dollars for the Frances Parrish story. Ambrose had not only rejected his proposal but also had run off a big, damp proof of the headimes and presented it to him.

"Take it to the general," he said. "Tell him to roll his cannon down here and challenge me, if he's up to it. But he'll be up against two of us now, as well as the sheriff, if he ever wangles that warrant."

But Stockard did not appear. Not like him, thought Henry.

Ambrose laid down his stick of type, rubbed his eyes, and went to a little wood stove in the back. He had put coffee on, and now poured the black stuff into two stained crockery cups and set them on the composing stone.

He climbed onto a high stool, and Henry took one across the stone table from him and sat there flexing his fingers, as the editor scribbled words on the stone, then rubbed them away with a rag and tried other words. Finally he dropped his pencil and sat back.

" 'The Two Lives of Black Jack Logan,' " he said. "What think?"

"Fine. I was kind of mulling — this is just an idea," Henry said apologetically. "Something about Lazarus. You know, the man in the Bible who —"

"I know who Lazarus was! Jesus, Henry, give me credit! Give me credit! But maybe . . . how about 'Captain Lazarus: His Two Lives'?"

"No, I think Black Jack should be in the title."

"I agree." Ambrose looked at the clock. "Tell me about receiving the letter."

"Well, it was about two years ago, and the return address read, 'Juan Lucero, Hacienda Logano, Sta. Barbara, Costa Rica.' But there was a picture, too, and I looked at that first. Lucero? I didn't know any Lucero. Logan? Funny, so close to my own name. Well, the photograph showed a fine white house behind an iron fence — with Señor Lucero, apparently, standing in the gate. He had a white mustache but his hair looked pretty black. And he was skinny — looked tubercular. My father was Black Irish, and in a white suit and planter's hat, he could look the part of a Spaniard. It was him, all right.

"He looked sick, though. He looked like me after the mosquito finished with me. Very much like me! I think I knew right then, in my heart, that it was my father. . . ."

Henry had to stop talking. Feelings had been piling up in him like clothes in a closet, unsuspected because out of sight, and now there was a possibility of his being buried in grief when the door opened. He sipped coffee to get his throat clear.

Ambrose said, "Steady. Sentimentality is the curse of the Irish. Had tears before they had Busmill's."

Henry resumed. "All right. When I noticed what he had in his hand, I knew for damn sure it was Dad. He was holding a silver piccolo!" Ambrose shot another look at the clock. "One minute, Henry."

"He said that after the gang left, he looked at the horrible mess inside the barn, and there wasn't much left of the men's bodies. They'd been pretty well cremated. You couldn't tell one from another — but the brass buttons and so forth were there. So he laid his silver bars in some coals for a while, put them where one of the men's shoulder bars would have been, and let him pass for Black Jack.

"The soldier they reported had been dragged off and tortured somewhere was Dad. He took the payroll and left."

"*Why?* It's so damned fascinating! Hurry up — we've got to get back to work."

"Because the Army had cheated him out of a life as a musician and a bandleader, what he always wanted to be. And here God — his word, not mine — had saved him for another, happier life! 'For what purpose?' he said. The way he read it, God wanted him to have that career! So he took the money and left. He wandered down the coast, and when he reached the mountains of Costa Rica, he said it felt like home.

"He bought a little coffee *finca* and discovered he had another talent — farming. He did very well."

"You did say he was dying?"

"Yes. Tuberculosis. He said it was a matter of weeks . . ."

Someone rattled the knob. The door was locked for reasons of safety. Ambrose peeked through the blinds before letting in Sheriff "Whispering George" Bannock.

The big man accepted coffee, pressed his fingertips to his eyelids, and cleared his throat with obvious pain. They waited until his anguished croak finally came.

"I just went up to Cemetery Hill to tell Stockard. Never shoot that damned cannon again."

"What about the warrant, for God's sake?" Ambrose pleaded. "The old loony will kill us if he isn't locked up — or we'll have to kill him"

"Judge Scott. Studying report. Four pages."

"Stage fright." Ambrose snorted. "Well, did you tell Stockard maybe he'd better take off for Sonora? Is that why the stalling?"

"No. He'd already left! Emily apologized."

"Where was Milo?"

"Spider Ranch. Took the cannon."

Henry and Ambrose looked at each other in shock. *He took the damned cannon?* " Henry shouted.

"According to Emily. And it shore ain't in his front yard anymore."

Henry closed his eyes and tried to think like the general. Charge! — all Stockard knew. Attack, intimidate, bully. Must have lost hundreds of men that way. Impatience was his weakness. Arrogance — nobody as smart as he was. He must plan to seize the ranch house, like the small fort it was, and dare them to put it off. While Beckwith hired lawyers and set out to bleed Frances of any cash she had left.

The rest of his thinking he did in motion. He had brought his Winchester to the office, thinking they might well need to defend themselves. He made sure it was fully loaded, thinking with Stockard's mind some more — ambush? It was a strong possibility that it had been he who had fired the threatening shot on the road the other day. He made up his mind to stay off the road where possible, proceed fast but with prudence.

He noticed that the general's guidon was gone from the wall: this seemed to confirm all his suspicions. *You are in an unmistakable, if limited, military action, Sergeant.*

"Sheriff," he said, "why not tell the Grand Army men what's happening? Shake the saloons for a few more men, and get them out there to the Parrish ranch. I'll lead off as point man, right now, and beat the brush for traps. He's probably forted up in the ranch house. I don't know, though — he may try to trade his hostage for a run to the border."

"What hostage?"

"Frances Parrish. She stayed out there yesterday."

As he rode up the dark road in the warm night, he ran through the situation as they used to do when the captain would say, *"Take Hill 109."* He recalled that Frances had said there were tons of dried and salted foods there, and the old foul spring was inside the walled yard of the kitchen, so Stockard could withstand a siege. But if he wanted to try to escape to Mexico, of course, he had a hostage. But hell, Henry didn't care if he went all the way to Costa Rica, like his father, if he wanted to. Just don't hurt Frances!

He fought down the urge to spur the horse, knowing there was only one way to reach her, and that was by letting the horse travel at a reasonable gait.

The horse heard the sounds first, his ears pointing at the brush from which the wild noises were coming, and the dun sidled, indicating, *Want to check out that thicket?* In three seconds Henry was off the horse and lying under it with his rifle at his shoulder.

The racket became a frantic uproar barbed with oaths and sobs of fury. "God! Damn! Horse! I should have — damned idiot brush — ouch! Son of a bitch!"

From a thicket of the terible, fishhooked, wait-a-bit brush, a man stumbled onto the road, sobbing with rage and exhaustion. He fell to his hands and knees and was resting on all fours, gasping, when he saw the horse's hooves before him. His head raised and he looked up and saw the dun.

He staggered to his feet. "Miracle! Thank

you, Jesus! Stand easy, horse — easy there — easy now —"

"That's good advice, Gorman," Henry said. "Stand real easy or I'll blow you in two."

Budge's head swiveled back and forth. "I ain't got a gun!" he cried. "I lost it. Who is that?"

"It's Logan. What's going on, Budge? Sit down on the road and keep perfectly still. I have your head in my sights. Where are you coming from?"

"Hey, Logan? I got something for you! Right here! The general wrote it down for you."

Henry knelt under the horse, his saddle gun reacting to Gorman's every move, its front sight moving like a snake's head. "Where's your horse?" he demanded.

"I run him to death. Had to go clean out to Spanish Church, and then turn aroun' an' come back an' find you. I been walking and running since . . . here! Take this stuff — I've got to go on and wait at the stable for the general. . . ."

"Crawl up to the horse and lay it on the ground."

Gorman crawled, flat on his belly, to the shadow of the horse, laid some papers there, and wriggled back the same way. "Is he at Spider Ranch?" asked Henry.

"Uh-huh. Jesus, you don't have a bottle, do you?"

"No. What's going on out there?"

"Well," Gorman said, "he's took it over. The woman is okay. He won't hurt her."

"That's nice. I'm going to light a lamp — sit tight or I'll kill you. Understand, Budge?"

Henry rose and got the small Army field lamp from a saddlebag. The torch resembled a tiny metal pitcher, a wick coming from the spout. He knelt down, got it lighted, and spread the two papers on the earth. One was a map, the other a message covering the entire sheet of note paper and resembling a military dispatch. He read the last paragraph first and knew that he had to go alone to Spanish Church.

The dispatch read:

SUBJECT: Disposal of prisoner
TO: Logan, Henry, Sgt. U.S.A., ret.
FROM: Stockard, Milo, Brig. Gen.,
    U.S.A.,

1. This detachment has taken prisoner a female Caucasian twenty-two years old known as Frances Wingard Parrish. She must be disposed of as summarily as pos-

sible before this CP is struck and relocated.

2. Subject female will be released unharmed under the following conditions:

a. Sgt. Logan shall come, *alone and armed*, to the cemetery at the place known as Spanish Church, by 0500 hours tomorrow.

b. He shall signal his arrival by firing a shot.

c. At 0530 hours, a shot will be fired, informing Sgt. Logan that subject female has been released.

d. The entire area will then be off-limits to all save Sgt. Logan and Genl. Stockard.

e. At sunrise, the truce shall end and the adversaries may fire at will. Contest shall end upon the death of either man. If Sgt. Logan is killed, Genl. Stockard agrees to leave his beloved country and never return. If the general is killed, his widow shall pay for the erection of a plaque to mark the place of his death.

f. If anyone other than Sgt. Logan enters the area, he will be shot. This includes ranchers, miners, travelers, and smugglers, and the condition is without time limit.

g. Finally, if Sgt. Logan does not come to the designated spot by 1600 hours, the prisoner will be executed. Conditions described in (f) will then obtain, in perpetuity.

"Turn around, Gorman. Face the brush." He got up and made sure Budge was not armed. "Now take your boots off. I'll leave them a half mile up the road."

"You can't —"

"What's this map?" Henry shook it at him.

"Oh — I wasn't supposed to give you that. It's where his new command post is going to be."

Henry held it to the light, noticing at the bottom of the page the word DESTROY. *Tactical error, General! Did you forget Budge can't read? Wait a minute, though. The man is a fox. Did he really want me to get the map, to set me up for an ambush?*

"What do you know about the new CP?" he asked Gorman. "What's out there?"

"Parrish's gun. Where its marked on the map . . . little drawing of a rifle?"

Henry saw it, an inch-long lever-action rifle.

The details painstakingly drawn and shaded by a man trying to think something out? "And the rifle is his CP? Doesn't make sense."

"Does to him. Hey Logan, about my boots — I'll board your horse free for six months if —"

"No. Is she all right?"

"Yeah. She just set there reading a book and playing a mandolin."

"What was he going to do with her?"

"Never said a damned word about it."

Henry shouted, "Then why is he holding her?"

"Don't know, Logan! He never said."

Henry took himself in hand. "All right. I'm going on now. Does this trail you're coming in on go direct to the CP? Better tell me straight — the general is waiting there for me."

"Yes, only I lost it about where my horse keeled over. You'll see him. Pick it up there."

"Some men'll be coming along soon. This is very important: Tell them to go to the ranch and stay there. But not to go to the command post! Understand that?"

"I understand, Henry."

"What are you to tell them?"

"Not to go to the CP. Stay at the ranch."

"Good. Take this message from the general, and when you see the men, tell them to read it carefully. They'll under why they must, under no conditions, go out there. What are you to tell them?"

"Stay at the ranch! I ain't dumb, Logan."

No, you're way past dumb, thought Henry. *You're crazy.*

Chapter Twenty-Six

After a first, agonized vision of Frances as a hostage — bound, gagged, and blindfolded, terrified as she waited to hear the rattle of a gun bolt — Henry refused point-blank the possibility of her being hurt in any way. He put all his energies into reaching the church before dawn.

It was a quarter to nine when he left the road, and Gorman said it had taken him four hours to ride to where he had hit the wagon road. But Gorman had killed his horse, so he'd better count on five or six hours at a reasonable gait. Even a steady jog should see him in the wash below the church by two or three A.M.

Now and then one of the horses's shoes would strike a stone and sparks would fly, and the big red dun would stumble and recover its balance. The mountain night was still and clear and utterly silent, the sky blazing with hard, blue-white stars and a phosphorescent Milky Way. A sweetish smell rose from the brush and nighthawks flicked past.

When he thought of Frances again, he took an angry swipe at a scrub oak with his carbine.

A moment later the dun sidled and began making nervous snorts. Henry talked to it, dug his thumb into the big nerve on its withers, working it past the dead animal lying half in and half out of the brush. The horse settled down but he thought, *What if he gives out? What if he falls and breaks a leg? Breaks mine, too?*

To settle himself down, he tried to concentrate on the general and the insane duel they would fight at dawn.

For some reason he had no doubt that as far as ground rules went, Stockard would make a clean fight. Feeling so sure of his tactical superiority, he had no need to cheat. But once they touched swords —

He thought again of the general's conditions for releasing Frances, and realized his claim to tactical skill was legitimate: Thought it seemed rash to stay around and lure his adversary into a duel, knowing that in a day or two a posse would consider Frances dead, and close in on him, he had created a situation entirely within his control.

The object was to prove himself superior

to the Kansas City gunsmith, both as a sharp-shooter and a tactician. So, with too little time for a prolonged cat-and-monse hunt, the problem had been to get them both into a small area. Otherwise, considering the vastness of the dueling ground, the stalking could go on for days.

The arena he had chosen was the ground around the cemetery. Henry would have to stay close to it until he knew that Frances had been released. But that would be so close to dawn that be would not dare crawl around among dry branches and loose rock and risk being picked off as he sought strategic leverage.

Stockard had him where he wanted him — and the duel had not even started.

His own advantage, he reckoned, was that he had acquired the map — knew where Stockard's alleged "command post" was located — where a second gun would be hidden. Yet even that might be part of the general's cunning: feeding him false information. And why the hell, he wondered, should Stockard bother with a second gun? To set in motion some bizarre tactic he had been dreaming of for years?

Henry swore. Trying to decode the message of the map was like cracking walnuts with his teeth. Yet that second rifle had to have some special meaning to Stockard — be part of a maneuver so original that it would go down in military history as Stockard's Gambit, a trick to make it absolutely clear that for strategy he was right up there with Leonidas at Thermopylae.

However! Had he forgotten that Budge Gorman couldn't read? That he couldn't have understood the underlined word, DESTROY, at the bottom of the map? In this case, it would be Henry who had the advantage. . . .

If . . .

By midnight he was in the brushy canyons and stony ridges south of the church. Since the general had no idea from which direction his opponent would be coming, it seemed unlikely that he would be hoping to spring an ambush.

Henry managed to read his watch by starlight, and figured that with luck he would have a half hour of darkness in which to find the trap, test its teeth, try to fathom why it was there.

West of the church, the wash bottlenecked down and the hills on both sides overhung the little stream. The hillsides were dotted with small trees and rocks which in the darkness were almost indistinguishable. He rode through them with care, his head swiveling back and forth like an owl's.

But when he reached the bottom of the wash, he found it too brushy to ride. The stream itself was choked in manzanita thickets. He would crawl downstream through them if necessary, but the dun could not crawl, so he left him on the hillside above the thickets, tied him so that he could not wander in and spoil the chess game.

He put the gun on safety before entering the thickets. A twig could fire a gun as well as a man's finger. Moving with care, he twisted and crawled a passage through the brittle manzanita. Underfoot were rocks and a mat of dry leaves. Once he was blocked by a manzanita branch he could not get over, under, or through. He started whittling on it, but manzanita was tough wood, and he spent ten minutes cutting through it. Finally he was able to bend it cautiously and break the last few fibers. He moved the branch aside and crawled on.

The streambed grew dry; the creek had gone underground. Every few yards he had to stop, hold his breath, and listen. Then he would struggle a little farther through the thicket. The tension he felt was exactly like that of a night patrol. Finally he felt his feet getting cold and wet, and knew the stream had resurfaced.

That meant he had reached the crossing below the church.

He rose to his feet and took a long, painstaking look at the cliffs. High above, on his left, the cliff leaned away from the gorge, and he knew the ruins were up there.

A stone's throw ahead, the thickets ended, and he could see the shine of water in the middle of the sandy wash. Foot by foot, with held breath, he moved downstream until the sniper's dome was on his right. Stockard would not be up there tonight. Though the butte commanded the whole county, he had no spotter this time to guide his shots.

He was down here somewhere. Or up in the cemetery; or in the church. Or would he consider Rip's stone house a good ambuscade? And what about the mine?

He felt a powerful foreboding that the man was close, and he slipped the safety off the carbine and, still in the middle of the stream, went to one knee. He was now technically behind enemy lines. The challenger had had all night to stretch his trip wires and set his traps, and the darkness was profound. He rose to steal further downstream, breathing shallowly and with extreme care and moving with exaggerated caution. Chilled and soaked, each foot explored the sand before setting itself.

There was a sudden, eerie change in the

feel of the air. He halted.

The sound of a breeze in the piñon trees was part of the difference, for the feeling of being enclosed had lessened. Was he feeling and hearing the meadowlike opening of the side canyon? He felt sure he was. From here on he was like an infantry point man whose sole job was to attract enemy fire.

A few steps more and he stood exactly where Stockard had sketched the rifle on the map for his illiterate messenger. He knelt on the sand and raised his head. Overhead the sky was black, but above the cliffs it bleached down to a cold bottle-green. Holding his watch inches from his eyes, he could just make out the time: five o'clock. He was late. He should now be in the cemetery, firing a shot to let the general know he accepted his terms.

He stole a few minutes more to search among the small shrubs and rocks at the edge of the stream. He bumped into a log he re-membered, and wondered if the gun might lie on it. But his groping hands found nothing. Now the eastern horizon had lightened to a pale apricot. Crouching, he stared at the camp until he could make out the stump and, after that the fire ring took shape, and then the rock house beneath the cliff. He had his beaarings, and he turned to leave. But as he did so, he stepped on something in the water and sprawled in the shallows. His Winchester clattered on the stones. He waited for a shot from the general's ambuscade.

A woman screamed: *"Henry — no!"*

Swearing, he scrambled to his knees, his rifle dripping but at the ready. Her voice had come from the camp area. He supposed she was tied there, perhaps to the very stump on which her husband had died.

Then the general's voice barked, from somewhere beyond the camp: "Madam, if you raise your voice again, I'll have to kill you! Do you understand?"

"Understand —!"

Henry put the sounds together and decided that Stockard was barricaded behind the wall; that Frances was tied somewhere in the camp. It was impossible in this light to find either of them, so his only choice was to dance to Stockard's tune.

But first he looked for the thing on which he had tripped, and found it: Rip Parrish's rifle, engraved bejeweled, and wet. His fingers roved it, read the LET 'ER RIP! engraving, found the gun cocked, and finally left it exactly where he had found it — in Stockard's command post.

Henry stumbled through rocks and brush to the cemetery trail, blundering noisily up the cliff to the blighted little orchard. He went through the dead trees to the grave yard, where he stoped to get his breath, gazing down on the wash as a few landmarks emerged from the darkness. Then he pointed his carbine into the sky and fired a shot. A covey of doves exploded from a thick et near him in a startling, whistling explosion.

Now it was his turn to wait, sitting on a stone cross with his rifle across his knees. According to the general's conditions, he was now to release his hostage. Henry thought he would. Finding the Winchester had convinced him that Stockard intended to follow his own plan of battle.

He replaced the spent shell in his gun and watched small feathery clouds turn pink across the sky, listened to birds coming to life, and began to see the details of the camp below him. The cold gray picture taking shape reminded him of the moments before an attack — watching the place where you feared to go but were going nevertheless. There was a familiar empty feeling at the pit of his stomach.

Now, below the bluff, a big-bored rifle roared. The sound of it made Henry grin — it was the modified '85 Winchester with its big charge of powder and heavy bullet. He saw the flash, too, and nothing modest about it, either. It told him that the general was barricaded behind the stone wall beyond the camp. He had, if his word was good, released Frances, and was inviting Henry to move in on him. Keeping his eye on the wall, Henry started from rock to rock down the cliff trail. With the light still so dim, such caution seemed unnecessary. But the Hunter and his eye were no mean combination.

Near the bottom of the cliff, a black, volcanic ridge cut across the trail, low and uneven and resembling the ruin of an ancient fortification. Henry settled himself behind it and began fussily, soldier-fashion, to rearrange the furniture. He needed a rifle loop, so he stacked a couple of flat stones together and peered through it at the scene below. The wash appeared quiet and pretty, birds taking baths in the shallow water, the trees obscuring much of the camp but the executioner's chair standing out boldly.

Then he uttered a yelp and ducked.

A bullet had ripped across his barricade and smashed into a small tree just behind him; he heard the big boom of the shot an instant later. Birds near him flew into the brush. A large animal, probably a deer, clattered down the wash. He huddled behind the rocks, stealing glimpses of the wall. Judging by the heavy smoke drifting from them, Stockard was firing black powder, which probably meant his sweetheart gun. The old savage must like the smell of black powder, its slow, sure power; and perhaps the memories it brought — the nostalgia of the old Apace-killing days. . . .

Henry laid the rifle barrel in its loophole and lined up the iron sights for a return shot; saw dust fly from the six-inch gray stone he had aimed at, a safe two feet from the general's eyepiece.

And grinned as Stockard fired back — two feet above his head. Yes. by God, he thought, this will make a dandy story for Ben Ambrose, practically unbelievable: Two grown men, qualified snipers, firing at each other at a perfectly reasonable bull's-eye distance — but taking great care not to hurt each other!

After the general's next careful bull's-eye, Henry ripped off a fusillade of five roaring shots, filling the general's ambuscade with dust and ricocheting lead. He waited for his reply, and when it came, it was high again. He turned his head and looked behind him, and by God the slug had hit precisely where every shot was going home — a knot on the trunk of a little hackberry tree up the slope! The ten-ring every time.

After Stockard's next shot — damned near finishing off the tree with this one — Henry sprawled from rock to rock down the slope and set himself up behind a couple of boulders. Stockard threw a hasty shot through the manzanita brush at his left. Henry then gave him four shots back. Being careful not to hurt him.

Then, by infantry rushes, he worked on down the slope another fifty feet. A giant gray stone protruded from the slope at this point, a good fifteen feet high. Henry clambered up a piñon tree behind the boulder, and from it, he crawled out onto the rock. The view from the top was a sniper's dream. He could sweep the rock wall so completely that if any part of Stockard's anatomy got more than four feet from the wall, he could tear a hole in it.

In fact, a moment after he settled down to wait, he saw a boot moving on the ground. He adjusted his sights a hair. His target was a hoarhound weed a couple of feet to the right of Stockard's boot. He tore out the weed on the first try, and the general's foot disappeared. Then he pumped several more shots into the same area and, as the echoes and whining ricochets died, cupped his hands around his mouth and shouted: "Don't make me kill you, General! You're pinned down."

"Go to hell!" Stockard yelled back, firing a hurried shot to reinforce his determination. A yard away, the dust flew.

Henry felt a thrill. It was like suddenly finding yourself speaking a foreign language —

understanding something you really hadn't thought yourself capable of.

"General," he shouted, "you're finished. The sheriff is bringing a posse. And you don't have a hostage now. It's man-to-man."

"If you cross that stream, Logan," Stockard roared back, "you're a dead one!"

"I don't mean to cross it! I've got a box of shells and the Grand Army is a-coming! You're the one who's going to cross it — and surrender. Think it over."

"I kept my word!" Stockard shouted back. "I released the woman." A hesitation, then: "What are your terms?"

Henry's teeth showed in a fierce grin. *You're a piss-poor liar, my friend,* he thought. *You've still got your trap, and you think I'm playing right into it.*

"My terms are that you'll get an Army court-martial," he called back, "just like any soldier! Throw your rifle over the wall and stand up."

He was surprised by what happened next.

A yellow-and-black pennant appeared above the wall and waved back and forth. He had seen it in the office of the *Globe,* the general's old headquarters guidon.

Henry took aim and shot the staff in two.

"You bastard!" the general shouted.

But he stood up, his arms crossed, smoking

one of his bitter little cigars. Across his chest, two bandoliers were draped. He was wearing no eye patch.

I really should shoot him now, Henry thought. If he should get away, God knew what kind of depredations the savage would inflict on the people around there before he'd be corraled, and he could outhide a wildcat. But he owed something to those forty dead Apaches, too. Only complete and utter humiliation could satisfy Henry. Stockard on display behind bars.

"Stand fast!" Henry shouted.

He scrambled down the hillside, never taking his eyes off the grizzled warrior, reaching the cobbled beach short of the stream and stopping there to yell: "Advance to your side of the water and wait there."

He waited ten yards from the water, keeping the warm-barreled '95 gun on the old man, the steel about the temperature of body heat, watching Stockard clamber over the stone wall and, guidon over his shoulder, walk cockily past the first oak, skirt Parrish's fire ring, and pass the big juniper stump without a glance at it.

The general followed orders, halting short of the water. In an act of meaningless bravado, he worked the broken staff of his bumblebee guidon into the sand, setting up his command post — right where it had been on the map.

Henry let his gun barrel point above his man's head, as if it would be in bad taste to threaten a prisoner; even display a lack of confidence in himself.

"All right, General. I now ask you to cross the stream and wait on this side. When you reach the dry sand, turn your back to me."

Stockard advanced slowly into the water like a convert about to be baptized. He puffed on his cigar as he came. Now he was at the spot marked with an X on the map, the log lying like an alligator in the water, only a foot above the surface. He hesitated, seemed to be trying to decide whether to step over the log or go around it. Then he tripped, tried to catch himself, but fell flat in the water behind the log. For a moment he could not be seen in the geyser of muddy water.

Stockard's head reappeared above the log, his body underwater, his hat floating down the stream, and his bald head gleaming. Rip Parrish's carbine was in his hands, dripping wet as it came up from where Gorman had hidden it beside the log.

"Remember Wounded Knee!" he shouted.

He fired four shots, working the loading lever so fast that it was several seconds before he realized the gun was not firing — that there was no sound, no smoke. Henry put a shot into the water near him, to let him taste the cup a little deeper. Stockard reared to his knees and shook water from the rifle, swearing. Then he tried several times more to make the carbine talk, thinking, probably, that surely there was at least one dry shell in the loading tube.

At last he lowered the carbine, panting, and stared at Henry. Waiting for the secret to be revealed.

Henry reached in his pocket and tossed a handful of paraffineded cartridge into the water a few feet from the general. "Thought I'd better draw your teeth, General," he said. "Gorman gave me the map. Throw the gun here."

Stockard began swearing, sloshing and stumbling forward with the gun held over his shoulder like a club. He would keep walking, Henry supposed, until he was shot. So he raised his carbine and sent a shot into the gun butt and took it out of the general's hands.

He said: "General, I won't kill you, so you might as well give up. I'll shoot an arm, and then a leg, and then another arm, if I have to. I will cut you absolutely to pieces. Come forward and lie down on the sand."

Stockard, twenty feet away now, stared blankly at him. "Logan," he said, "you'd better shoot me, because I ain't beat. Always knew I'd die before a firing squad somewhere.

Shoot, you son of a bitch!"

Henry shook his head. Stockard put his hand to the back of his neck and rubbed it like a very tired, defeated man. But a moment afterward, Henry saw the flash of the steel in his hand and knew he had drawn a throwing knife. He fired and Stockard swore and hugged his bloody hand to his belly, his chest heaving.

Henry said, "Well, General, shall we wrestle? I think I can take you."

Stockard bent and groped in the bloody water around his ankles, and when he straightened, he held the knife in his left hand. He started toward Henry with the knife raised.

Henry realized then that he was not only courageous but also insane. But still, with the old Logan reluctance to kill something that might be made into a pet or a friend, he decided on a final stratagem.

"General," he said, "you've put up a brave and soldierly fight. I respect you for it. I haven't always agreed with your tactics, but I admire you as a soldier. I ask you now to surrender your weapon and your command."

Stockard breathed like a foundered horse. The water was running down his shirt, and blood streamed from his hand and began coloring the water. He looked down at it, seemed fascinated. He raised his eyes to Henry and said, "Everything I did, Henry, was done to honor your father."

"I appreciate that," Henry said. "And I'm sure he would have. I'll see that your guidon is preserved at Fort Bowie, sir. Will you surrender your weapon and your command?"

Stockard reversed the knife, holding it by the point, and began walking, sloshing on through the bloody water. He halted two paces from Henry and offered his knife, then stood fast.

"By God, Logan," he said, "you're a soldier, after all. I am honored to surrender to you."

"Did you ask him if he killed Rip?" Henry asked Frances.

"Oh, he told me! He seemed so proud of it. He told me all the boring details you bored me with before. Guns!"

"If they hadn't been invented," Henry told her, "mankind would be carrying some of the damnedest bows and arrows you can imagine!"

It was evening. Frances had already bored him with one of her papa's favorite lines from Tennyson, something about the long day waning and the slow moon climbing, and from where they sat in the big parlor of the ranch house, they could see it climbing above the hills east of the ranch, thin and crisp as an ice design on a window. They were exhausted, having ridden for an hour before making contact with the posse heading for Spanish Church. Then, before they could ride on to the ranch, Henry had had to explain to them where General Stockard would be found — manacled to a large stump in Rip Parrish's camp.

Frances had been able to stanch the bleeding of his hand, and he had made it a point to betray no pain whatever as she cleaned the hole with a powerful antiseptic. The parting was very formal: a salute by Henry; a nod by the manacled prisoner; a grave statement by Frances, thanking him for not having hurt her, and releasing her according to his promise.

"Madam," he'd told her, "I am an officer of the old school. We respect women and keep our word."

"Of course," Henry reminded him, "it's your sworn duty as a soldier to attempt to escape as soon as we leave you. But I'm taking all the weapons."

"You'd be a damned poor soldier if you didn't."

Frances had protested, but Henry was having a drop of Bushmill's behind his quinine, and she was having a drop of Rip's wine. In the kitchen, Josefina and Alejandro were chat-

318

tering as they washed the dishes. Henry waved his glass at the room in general.

"It's a fine place you have, Miss Frances," he said. "But it's my belief you need to get away from it for a while."

"I intend to."

"And I don't mean Hermosillo, Panchita. According to my father's letter, I have a little place down in Costa Rica."

"They have a little yellow fever down in Costa Rica, too."

"Only in the lowlands, and my father's coffee plantation is in the highlands. I'll show you the picture of the house and garden when I get my stuff from Allie's. He said there are butterflies there a foot across!"

"And I've heard tell the anopheles mosquito is so big, it's the national bird!"

"But if you read the *Globe,* " Henry said, "you'll know that I can take the ash off a mosquito's cigarette at a hundred yards. So there's nothing to worry about."

THORNDIKE-MAGNA hopes you have enjoyed this Large Print book. All our Large Print titles are designed for easy reading, and all our books are made to last. Other Thorndike Press or Magna Print books are available at your library, through selected bookstores, or directly from the publishers. For more information about current and upcoming titles, please call or mail your name and address to:

THORNDIKE PRESS
P.O. Box 159
Thorndike, Maine 04986
(800) 223-6121
(207) 948-2962 (in Maine and Canada call collect)

or in the United Kingdom:

MAGNA PRINT BOOKS
Long Preston, Near Skipton
North Yorkshire,
England BD23 4ND
(07294) 225

There is no obligation, of course.